Mary Carlyle Aitken Carlyle

Scottish Song

A Selection of the Choicest Lyrics of Scotland

Mary Carlyle Aitken Carlyle

Scottish Song
A Selection of the Choicest Lyrics of Scotland

ISBN/EAN: 9783744777001

Printed in Europe, USA, Canada, Australia, Japan

Cover: Foto ©Andreas Hilbeck / pixelio.de

More available books at **www.hansebooks.com**

SCOTTISH SONG

A SELECTION OF THE

CHOICEST LYRICS OF SCOTLAND

COMPILED AND ARRANGED, WITH BRIEF NOTES

BY

MARY CARLYLE AITKEN

London

MACMILLAN AND CO.

1874

CONTENTS.

PREFACE.

The peculiar merits of the Songs of Scotland have so often been insisted upon, that little remains for me here, except to point out what my aim has been in adding one more to the already long list of printed collections. Hitherto compilers have studied to have quantity rather than quality; there is not a sufficient number of really excellent Scottish Songs, exclusive of Burns's, to fill more than a small volume; so that the wheat has in few cases been separated from the chaff. I have inserted no song except such as I believed to be possessed of real merit; and, at the same time, have chosen only those that have won their way to the hearts of the Scottish people, and dwelt there,—in itself a good test, for, as Goethe says, 'What has kept its place in the hearts of the people even for twenty years is pretty certain to have true merit.'

'The smallness of the space at my command, while allowing me to exclude such as I deemed inferior, has compelled me to leave out many excellent songs of Burns, whose name will be lovingly cherished as long as there are Scotch hearts in the world. Mr. Carlyle says of him, ' It will seem a small praise if we rank him as the first of all our song-writers ; for we know not where to find one worthy of being second to him.' I should have preferred to make these songs the foundation of this collection, but they have been so often printed, and are so well known, that it has been thought advisable to introduce them rather as a spice than as the *pièce de resistance.*

In the case of a few of the older songs, written in an age, as far as language is concerned at least, more rude than our own, where I have not been able to give the earliest versions entire, I have chosen to omit an indelicate stanza, when not destroying the sense, rather than substitute commonplace vulgarized readings of them. When there are changes they are for most part by the delicate masterly hand of Burns. When no author's name is affixed to a song, it is because it is unknown.

The notes, which have been made as short as possible, are given in the text, instead of at the end of the volume, and, it is hoped, may be more acceptable in that form.

The Songs are divided into four parts, and are classed, as will be seen, according to subject, not according to date, that arrangement being the only one practicable, for not only are the dates of many of the gems unknown, but even the names of their authors have perished.

In Part I. are such songs as are devoid, or almost devoid, of the comic element, viz.. serious love-songs, for most part lyrical, what Wordsworth would call 'Songs of the Affections,' an unsuitable name here, however, the Scotch being by nature a taciturn people, and mere affection seldom tempting them to sing.

In Part II. are social and drinking songs. with which latter Scotland is abundantly supplied. In this province, too, Burns has lavishly poured out his splendid genius, with a strange fatality, singing the praises of the Syren that lured him to his own ruin.

In Part III. are love-songs of another class than the first, admitting the comic and jovial element.

In Part IV. are Jacobite and war-songs.

I have tried, by careful reading, and by the use of all the opportunities in my power, to make an attractive volume of the really good songs of my native country. As to whether I have succeeded or failed, it is fit that the reader, not I, should be the judge.

M. C. A.

CHELSEA, *March, 1874.*

Part I.

Part I.

SCOTTISH SONG.

I.

CA' THE YOWES.

Ca' the yowes to the knowes,
Ca' them whare the heather grows,
Ca' them whare the burnie rows,
  My bonnie dearie.

As I gaed down the water side,
There I met my shepherd lad,
He row'd me sweetly in his plaid,
  And he ca'd me his dearie.

Will ye gang down the water side,
And see the waves sae sweetly glide
Beneath the hazels spreading wide,
  The moon it shines fu' clearly.

I was bred up at nae sic school,
My shepherd lad, to play the fool;
And a' the day to sit in dool,
  And naebody to see me.

A

Ye shall get gowns and ribbons meet,
Cauf leather shoon upon your feet,
And in my arms ye'se lie and sleep,
    And ye shall be my dearie.

If ye'll but stand to what ye've said,
I'se gang wi' you, my shepherd lad ;
And ye may row me in your plaid,
    And I shall be your dearie.

While waters wimple to the sea,
While day blinks in the lift sae hie ;
Till clay-cauld death shall blin' my e'e,
    Ye aye shall be my dearie.

"This beautiful song is in the true old Scotch taste."
—*Burns.*

II.

THE EWE BUGHTS.

Will ye gang to the ewe-bughts, Marion,
    And wear-in the sheep wi' me?
The sun shines sweet, my Marion,
    But no half sae sweet as thee.

O, Marion's a bonnie lass,
    And the blythe blink's in her e'e ;
And fain wad I marry Marion,
    Gin Marion wad marry me.

There's gowd in your garters, Marion,
   And silk on your white haus-bane;
Fu' fain wad I kiss my Marion,
   At e'en when I come hame.

There's braw lads in Earnslaw, Marion,
   Wha gape, and glower with their e'e,
At kirk when they see my Marion;
   But nane of them loves like me.

I've nine milk-ewes, my Marion,
   A cow and a brawny quey,
I'll gie them a' to my Marion,
   Just on her bridal-day.

And ye'se get a green sey apron,
   And waistcoat o' London broun;
And wow but ye'll be vap'rin'
   Whene'er ye gang to the toun.

I'm young and stout, my Marion,
   Nane dances like me on the green;
And gin ye forsake me, Marion,
   I'll e'en gae draw up wi' Jean.

Sae put on your pearlings, Marion,
   And kirtle o' cramasie;
And sune as my chin has nae hair on,
   I shall come west, and see ye.

"This sonnet appears to be ancient: that and its simplicity have recommended it to a place here."—*Percy's Reliques.*

III.

O'ER THE MOOR AMANG THE HEATHER.

Jean Glover.—Born 1758; Died 1801.

Coming through the craigs o' Kyle,
  Amang the bonnie blooming heather,
There I met a bonnie lassie,
  Keeping a' her ewes thegither.

    O'er the moor amang the heather,
      O'er the moor amang the heather;
    There I met a bonnie lassie,
      Keeping a' her ewes thegither.

Says I, my dear, where is thy hame,—
  In moor or dale, pray tell me whether?
She says, I tend the fleecy flocks
  That feed amang the blooming heather.

We laid us down upon a bank,
  Sae warm and sunny was the weather:
She left her flocks at large to rove
  Amang the bonnie blooming heather.

While thus we lay, she sang a sang,
  Till echo rang a mile and farther;
And aye the burden of the sang
  Was, o'er the moor amang the heather.

She charmed my heart, and aye sinsyne
  I couldna' think on ony ither;

By sea and sky, she shall be mine,
   The bonnie lass amang the heather !

O'er the moor amang the heather,
   Down amang the blooming heather,—
By sea and sky she shall be mine,
   The bonnie lass amang the heather!

Burns says that he wrote out the words of this song from the singing of the author—a girl, whose character does not concern us here—"as she was strolling through the country with a slight-of-hand blackguard."

IV.

THE LASS O' PATIE'S MILL.

Allan Ramsay.—Born 1686; Died 1757.

The lass o' Patie's Mill,
   Sae bonnie, blythe, and gay,
In spite of a' my skill,
   She stole my heart away.
When teddin' out the hay,
   Bareheaded on the green,
Love midst her locks did play,
   And wanton'd in her een.

Her arms, white, round, and smooth,
   Breasts in their rising dawn,
To age it would give youth,
   To press them with his han'.
Through all my spirits ran
   An ecstasy of bliss,
When I such sweetness fan'
   Wrapt in a balmy kiss.

Without the help of art,
    Like flowers that grace the wild,
She did her sweets impart,
    Whene'er she spak' or smiled :
Her looks they were so mild,
    Free from affected pride,
She me to love beguil'd,
    I wish'd her for my bride.

Oh ! had I a' the wealth
    Hopetoun's high mountains fill,
Insured lang life and health,
    And pleasure at my will ;
I'd promise, and fulfil,
    That nane but bonnie she,
The lass o' Patie's Mill,
    Should share the same wi' me.

Allan Ramsay, who, after Burns, may still be called the most distinguished Scottish poet, was born at Leadhills, in Lanarkshire, in 1686. His father, the manager of Lord Hopetoun's mines there, died soon after his son's birth. His mother having married again, Allan was apprenticed by his step-father to a wigmaker in Edinburgh, which career he continued till 1718, when he became a bookseller. He published a collection of Scottish songs, among which there are several of his own, called *The Tea Table Miscellany*. The first complete edition of it appeared in London in 1733. It is the parent of nearly all subsequent collections. Ritson and others have blamed him for his want of fidelity in editing some of the old songs ; but it is evident from the *polished* specimens, that it would have been impossible for him, even with his by no means narrow ideas on the subject, to print them without alterations or omissions. It is, of course, a pity that he did not more clearly mark the changes which he and the "ingenious young gentlemen" who helped in the task, had made.   Ramsay's *Gentle Shepherd* is thought, by competent judges, to be the most complete and beautiful of modern pastorals.   His son Allan was also a remarkable man; and his name is still well known as a portrait painter.

v.

THE BROOM OF COWDENKNOWS.

How blyth, ilk morn, was I to see
　My swain come o'er the hill !
He skipt the burn, and flew to me ;
　I met him with good will.

　　O, the broom, the bonnie, bonnie broom,
　　　The broom of the Cowdenknows !
　I wish I were wi' my dear swain,
　　Wi' his pipe, and my yowes.

I neither wanted yowe nor lamb,
　While his flocks near me lay :
He gather'd in my sheep at night,
　And cheer'd me a' the day.

He tuned his pipe and reed sae sweet,
　The birds sat list'ning by ;
E'en the dull cattle stood and gazed,
　Charm'd wi' his melody.

While thus we spent our time, by turns,
　Betwixt our flocks and play,
I envied not the fairest dame,
　Though e'er so rich and gay.

Hard fate ! that I should banish'd be,
   Gang heavily, and mourn,
Because I loved the kindest swain
   That ever yet was born.

He did oblige me every hour ;
   Could I but faithfu' be ?
He staw my heart ; could I refuse
   Whate'er he ask'd of me ?

My doggie, and my little kit,
   That held my wee sowp whey,
My plaidie, broach, and crooked-stick,
   Maun now lie useless by.

Adieu, ye Cowdenknows, adieu !
   Fareweel a' pleasures there !
Ye gods, restore me to my swain,
   It's a' I crave or care.

This and the following song are from *The Tea Table Miscellany*.

VI.

THE BROOM OF THE COWDEN-KNOWS.

Robert Crawford.—Born 1695 ? Died 1733.

When summer comes, the swains on Tweed
   Sing their successful loves.
Around the ewes and lambkins feed,
   And music fills the groves.

But my lov'd song is then the broom
　　So fair on Cowdenknows;
For sure, so sweet, so soft a bloom,
　　Elsewhere there never grows.

There Colin tuned his oaten reed,
　　And won my yielding heart;
No shepherd e'er that dwelt on Tweed,
　　Could play with half such art.

He sang of Tay, of Forth, and Clyde,
　　The hills and dales all round,
Of Leader-haughs, and Leader-side,
　　Oh! how I bless'd the sound.

Yet more delightful is the broom
　　So fair on Cowdenknows;
For sure, so fresh, so bright a bloom,
　　Elsewhere there never grows.

Not Teviot braes, so green and gay,
　　May with this broom compare;
Not Yarrow banks in flow'ry May,
　　Nor the bush aboon Traquair.

More pleasing far are Cowdenknows,
　　My peaceful happy home,
Where I was wont to milk my ewes,
　　At ev'n among the broom.

Ye powers that haunt the woods and plains
　　Where Tweed with Teviot flows,
Convey me to the best of swains,
　　And my loved Cowdenknows.

VII.

*THE WAUKING OF THE FAULD.**

Allan Ramsay.

My Peggy is a young thing,
  Just enter'd in her teens.
Fair as the day, and sweet as May,
Fair as the day, and always gay :
    My Peggy is a young thing,
      And I'm no very auld,
      Yet weel I like to meet her at
        The wauking of the fauld.

My Peggy speaks sae sweetly
  Whene'er we meet alane,
I wish nae mair to lay my care,
I wish nae mair o' a' that's rare :
    My Peggy speaks sae sweetly,
      To a' the lave I'm cauld ;
      But she gars a' my spirits glow
        At wauking of the fauld.

My Peggy smiles sae kindly
  Whene'er I whisper love,
That I look down on a' the town,
That I look down upon a crown :
    My Peggy smiles sae kindly,
      It makes me blyth and bauld,
      And naething gi'es me sic delight,
        As wauking of the fauld.

---

* Wauking the Fauld : watching the sheep-folds at
night during the season when the lambs are being weaned.

My Peggy sings sae saftly,
　When on my pipe I play;
By a' the rest it is confest,
By a' the rest that she sings best:
　My Peggy sings sae saftly,
　　And in her sangs are tauld,
　Wi' innocence the wale o' sense,
　　At wauking of the fauld.

VIII.

PEGGY AND PATIE.

Allan Ramsay.

Peggy.

When first my dear laddie gaed to the green hill,
And I at ewe-milking first say'd my young skill,
To bear the milk-bowie nae pain was to me,
When I at the bughting forgather'd with thee.

Patie.

When corn-riggs wav'd yellow, and blue heather-
　　bells
Bloom'd bonnie on moorland and sweet rising
　　fells,
Nae birns, briers, or bracken, gave trouble to me,
If I found but the berries right ripen'd for thee.

Peggy.

When thou ran, or wrestled, or putted the stane,
And cam' aff the victor, my heart was aye fain:
Thy ilka sport manly gave pleasure to me,
For nane can putt, wrestle, or run swift as thee.

Patic.

Our Jenny sings saftly the 'Cowden Broom-
        knowes,'
And Rosie lilts sweetly the 'Milking the Ewes,'
There's few 'Jenny Nettles' like Nancy can sing:
With, 'Through the wood, Laddie,' Bess gars
        our lugs ring:

But when my dear Peggy sings, with better skill,
The 'Boatman,' 'Tweedside,' or the 'Lass of
        the Mill,'
'Tis many times sweeter and pleasant to me;
For though they sing nicely, they cannot like thee.

Peggy.

How easy can lassies trow what they desire!
With praises sae kindly increasing love's fire:
Give me still this pleasure, my study shall be
To make myself better and sweeter for thee.

Peggy and Patie are the heroine and hero of the
Gentle Shepherd; from which this song, as well as the
one preceding it, is taken.

IX.

BONNIE CHRISTY.

Allan Ramsay.

How sweetly smells the simmer green!
    Sweet taste the peach and cherry;
Painting and order please our e'en,
    And claret makes us merry:

But finest colours, fruits and flowers,
  And wine, though I be thirsty,
Lose a' their charms, and weaker powers,
  Compared wi' those of Christy.

When wand'ring o'er the flow'ry park,
  No natural beauty wanting :
How lightsome is't to hear the lark,
  And birds in concert chanting !
But if my Christy tunes her voice,
  I'm rapt in admiration :
My thoughts wi' ecstasies rejoice,
  And drap the hale creation.

Whene'er she smiles a kindly glance,
  I take the happy omen,
And aften mint to make advance,
  Hoping she'll prove a woman.
But, dubious of my ain desert,
  My sentiments I smother,
Wi' secret sighs I vex my heart,
  For fear she love another.

Thus sang blate Edie by a burn,
  His Christy did o'erhear him ;
She doughtna let her lover mourn ;
  But, ere he wist, drew near him.
She spak' her favour wi' a look,
  Which left nae room to doubt her ;
He wisely this white minute took,
  And flang his arms about her.

My Christy ! witness, bonny stream
  Sic joys frae tears arising !

I wish this may na be a dream,
  O love the maist surprising !
Time was too precious now for tauk ;
  This point of a' his wishes
He wadna wi' set speeches bauk,
  But wared it a' on kisses.

Ramsay places this song first in *The Tea Table Miscellany ;* so, probably, it was his favourite.

X.

ROSLIN CASTLE.

Richard Hewitt.—Died 1764.

'Twas in that season of the year,
When all things gay and sweet appear,
That Colin, with the morning ray,
Arose and sung his rural lay.
Of Nanny's charms the shepherd sung :
The hills and dales with Nanny rung ;
While Roslin Castle heard the swain,
And echoed back his cheerful strain.

Awake, sweet Muse ! The breathing spring
With rapture warms : awake, and sing !
Awake and join the vocal throng,
And hail the morning with a song :
To Nanny raise the cheerful lay,
O ! bid her haste and come away ;
In sweetest smiles herself adorn,
And add new graces to the morn !

O look, my love ! on ev'ry spray
Each feather'd warbler tunes his lay :
'Tis beauty fires the ravish'd throng,
And love inspires the melting song :
Then let the raptur'd notes arise,
For beauty darts from Nanny's eyes ;
And love my rising bosom warms,
And fills my soul with sweet alarms.

Oh, come, my love ! Thy Colin's lay
With rapture calls, O come away !
Come while the muse this wreath shall twine
Around that modest brow of thine.
O hither haste, and with thee bring
That beauty blooming like the spring,
Those graces that divinely shine,
And charm this ravish'd heart of mine !

Burns speaks of the above as " beautiful verses."

XI.

TWEEDSIDE.

Attributed to Lord Yester.—Born 1645 ; Died 1713.

When Maggy and I were acquaint
  I carried my noddle fu' hie ;
Nae lintwhite in a' the gay plain,
  Nae gowdspink sae bonnie as she !
I whistled, I piped, and I sang ;
  I woo'd, but I cam' nae great speed :
Therefore I maun wander abroad,
  And lay my banes far frae the Tweed.

To Maggy my love I did tell;
My tears did my passion express:
Alas! for I lo'ed her ower weel,
And the women lo'e sic a man less.
Her heart it was frozen and cauld;
Her pride had my ruin decreed;
Therefore I maun wander abroad,
And lay my banes far frae the Tweed.

XII.

TWEEDSIDE.

R. Crawford.

What beauties does Flora disclose!
How sweet are her smiles upon Tweed!
Yet Mary's, still sweeter than those,
Both nature and fancy exceed.
Nor daisy nor sweet-blushing rose,
Not all the gay flowers of the field,
Not Tweed gliding gently through those,
Such beauty and pleasure does yield.

The warblers are heard in the grove,
The linnet, the lark, and the thrush,
The blackbird, and sweet-cooing dove,
With music enchant ev'ry bush.
Come, let us go forth to the mead,
Let us see how the primroses spring;
We'll lodge in some village on Tweed,
And love while the feather'd folks sing.

How does my love pass the long day?
  Does Mary not tend a few sheep?
Do they never carelessly stray,
  While happily she lies asleep?
'Tweed's murmurs should lull her to rest;
  Kind nature indulging my bliss,
To relieve the soft pains of my breast,
  I'd steal an ambrosial kiss.

"Tis she does the virgins excel,
  No beauty with her may compare;
Love's graces all round her do dwell;
  She's fairest, where thousands are fair.
Say, charmer, where do thy flocks stray,
  Oh! tell me at noon where they feed;
Shall I seek them on sweet-winding Tay
  Or the pleasanter banks of the Tweed.

Burns had been informed that the " Mary " of this song was a Mary Stewart of the Castlemilk family; Scott, on the other hand, says that she was a Mary Lillias Scott, daughter of Walter Scott. Esq. of Harden, and a descendant of the celebrated " Flower of Yarrow." It is now supposed that the latter opinion is the correct one.

XIII.

A RED, RED ROSE.

R. Burns.—Born 1759; Died 1796.

O, my luve's like a red, red rose,
  That's newly sprung in June,
O, my luve's like the melodic,
  That's sweetly play'd in tune.

B

As fair art thou, my bonnie lass,
  Sae deep in love am I ;
And I will love thee still, my dear,
  Till a' the seas gang dry.

Till a' the seas gang dry, my dear,
  And the rocks melt wi' the sun ;
O, I will love thee still, my dear,
  While the sands o' life shall run.

And fare thee weel, my only luve,
  And fare thee weel a while ;
And I will come again, my luve,
  Though it were ten thousand mile.

XIV.

OH! DINNA ASK ME GIN I LO'E THEE.

John Dunlop.—Born 1755 ; Died 1820.

Oh ! dinna ask me gin I lo'e thee ;
  Troth I dar'na' tell :
Dinna ask me gin I lo'e thee ;
  Ask it o' yoursel'.

Oh ! dinna look sae sair at me,
  For weel ye ken me true ;
O, gin ye look sae sair at me
  I dar'na' look at you.

When ye gang to yon braw, braw town,
  And bonnier lassies see,
O, dinna, Jamie, look at them,
  Lest you should mind na me.

For I could never bide the lass,
  That ye'd lo'e mair than me;
And O, I'm sure, my heart would break,
  Gin ye'd prove false to me.

XV.

IN YON GARDEN.

In yon garden fine and gay,
Picking lilies a' the day,
Gathering flowers o' ilka hue,
I wistna then what love could do.

Where love is planted there it grows;
It buds and blooms like any rose;
It has a sweet and pleasant smell;
No flower on earth can it excel.

I put my hand into the bush,
  And thought the sweetest rose to find;
But pricked my finger to the bone,
  And left the sweetest rose behind.

A very old fragment, first printed in *The Scots Musical Museum*, a well-known work (commenced 1787, completed 1803), which owes much of its worth to Burns, who generously helped Johnson, an engraver in Edinburgh, the editor and publisher of it, in his patriotic task. Burns, although admitting that it has defects, says of it, " I will venture to prophecy that, to future ages, your Publication will be the text-book and standard of Scottish Song and Music." Under the new and luminous editorship of Mr. David Laing (Blackwood and Sons, 1853), it now contains a copious, almost endless, mass of annotations, elucidations, and anecdotes of the songs and song-writers of Scotland.

XVI.

BESSY BELL AND MARY GRAY.

O Bessy Bell and Mary Gray,
   They war twa bonnie lasses !
They biggit a bower on yon burn brae,
   And theekit it o'er wi' rashes.
They theekit it o'er wi' rashes green,
   They theekit it o'er wi' heather,
But the pest cam frae the burrow's town
   And slew them baith thegither !

They thought to lie in Methven kirk-yard,
   Amang their noble kin,
But they maun lie in Stronach-Haugh,
   To biek forenent the sin.
And Bessy Bell and Mary Gray,
   They war twa bonnie lasses !
They biggit a bower on yon burn brae,
   And theekit it o'er wi' rashes.

"There is much tenderness and simplicity in these
verses."—*Walter Scott.*

According to tradition, Bessy Bell and Mary Gray were
two young ladies of Perthshire, who, at the time of the
plague (in 1645), retired for safety to some cottage or
"bower," about a mile from Lynedoch House, Mary
Gray's home. A youth, who was much attached to them,
supplied them with food from Perth, but at last brought
the infection, and they both died ; according to custom,
they were buried in a lonely spot, instead of with "their
noble kin."—For Ramsay's modern song on this subject
see p. 194.

XVII.

AN' THOU WERE MY AIN THING.

An' thou were my ain thing,
I would love thee, I would love thee;
An' thou were my ain thing,
　How dearly would I love thee!

Of race divine thou needs must be.
Since nothing earthly equals thee;
For heaven's sake, oh, favour me,
　Who only live to love thee.

The gods one thing peculiar have,
To ruin none whom they can save;
O, for their sake, support a slave,
　Who only lives to love thee.

To merit I no claim can make,
But that I love, and, for your sake,
What man can name I'll undertake,
　So dearly do I love thee.

My passion, constant as the sun,
Flames stronger still, will ne'er have done,
Till fate my thread of life have spun,
　Which breathing out, I'll love thee.

XVIII.

SHE IS A WINSOME WEE THING.

R. Burns.

She is a winsome wee thing,
She is a winsome wee thing,

She is a bonnie wee thing,
  This sweet wee wife o' mine !

I never saw a fairer,
I never loo'd a dearer ;
And neist my heart I'll wear her,
  For fear my jewel tine.

She is a winsome wee thing,
She is a handsome wee thing,
She is a bonnie wee thing,
  This sweet wee wife o' mine.

The world's wrak we share o't,
The warstle and the care o't ;
Wi' her I'll blythely bear it,
  And think my lot divine.

XIX.

O GIN MY LOVE.

O were my love yon lilac fair,
  Wi' purple blossoms to the spring,
And I a bird to shelter there,
  When wearied on my little wing.

How I wad mourn when it was torn,
  By autumn wild, and winter rude !
But I wad sing on wanton wing,
  When youthfu' May its bloom renew'd.

O gin my love were yon red rose,
  That grows upon the castle wa',

And I mysel' a drap o' dew,
  Into her bonnie breast to fa' !

O ! there beyond expression blest,
  I'd feast on beauty a' the night ;
Seal'd on her silk-saft faulds to rest,
  Till fley'd awa' by Phœbus' light.

The first two verses of this song are by Burns.

XX.

THE LASS OF BALLOCHMYLE.

R. Burns.

'Twas even,—the dewy fields were green,
  On every blade the pearls hang ;
The zephyr wanton'd round the bean,
  And bore its fragrant sweets alang ;
In ev'ry glen the mavis sang :
  All nature list'ning seem'd the while,
Except where greenwood echoes rang,
  Amang the braes o' Ballochmyle.

With careless step I onward stray'd,
  My heart rejoiced in nature's joy ;
When, musing in a lonely glade,
  A maiden fair I chanced to spy ;
Her look was like the morning's eye,
  Her air like nature's vernal smile ;
Perfection whisper'd, passing by,
  Behold the lass o' Ballochmyle !

Fair is the morn in flowery May,
  And sweet is night in Autumn mild,
When roving through the garden gay,
  Or wand'ring in the lonely wild;
But woman, nature's darling child!
  There all her charms she does compile;
Even there her other works are foil'd,
  By the bonny lass o' Ballochmyle.

Oh, had she been a country maid,
  And I the happy country swain,
Though shelter'd in the lowest shed
  That ever rose on Scotland's plain!
Through weary winter's wind and rain,
  With joy, with rapture, I would toil;
And nightly to my bosom strain
  The bonny lass o' Ballochmyle.

Then pride might climb the slippery steep,
  Where fame and honours lofty shine;
And thirst of gold might tempt the deep,
  Or downward dig the Indian mine.
Give me the cot below the pine,
  To tend the flocks, or till the soil,
And every day have joys divine,
  With the bonny lass o' Ballochmyle.

XXI.

BUSK YE, BUSK YE.

Allan Ramsay.

Busk ye, busk ye, my bonnie bride,
Busk ye, busk ye, my bonnie marrow,

Busk ye, busk ye, my bonnie bride,
And let us to the braes of Yarrow.
There will we sport and gather dew,
Dance while lav'rocks sing i' the morning ;
Then learn frae turtles to prove true,
O Bell, ne'er vex me with thy scorning !

To westlin' breezes Flora yields,
And when the beams are kindly warming,
Blytheness appears o'er all the fields,
And nature looks mair fresh and charming.
Learn frae the burns that trace the mead,
Though on their banks the roses blossom,
Yet hastily they flow to Tweed,
And pour their sweetness in his bosom.

Haste ye, haste ye, my bonnie Bell,
Haste to my arms, and there I'll guard thee ;
With free consent my fears repel,
I'll with my love and care reward thee.
Thus sang I saftly to my fair,
Wha rais'd my hopes with kind relenting.
O ! queen of smiles, I ask nae mair,
Since now my bonnie Bell's consenting.

The first four lines of this song are much older.

XXII.

WILLIE'S DROWNED IN YARROW.

Doun in yon garden sweet and gay,
  Where bonnie grows the lilie,
I heard a fair maid, sighing, say
  " My wish be wi' sweet Willie !

O Willie's rare, and Willie's fair,
   And Willie's wondrous bonny ;
And Willie hecht to marry me,
   Gin e'er he married ony.

Oh, gentle wind, that bloweth south,
   From where my love repaireth,
Convey a kiss frae his dear mouth,
   And tell me how he fareth !

O tell sweet Willie to come doun,
   And bid him no be cruel ;
And tell him no to break the heart
   Of his love and only jewel.

O tell sweet Willie to come doun,
   And hear the mavis singing ;
And see the birds on ilka bush,
   And leaves around them hinging.

The lav'rock there, wi' her white breist,
   And gentle throat so narrow ;
There's sport eneuch for gentlemen,
   On Leader Haughs and Yarrow.*

O Leader Haughs are wide and braid,
   And Yarrow Haughs are bonny ;
There Willie hecht to marry me,
   If e'er he married ony.

But Willie's gone, whom I thought on,
   And does not hear me weeping :

---

* *Leader Haughs :* the valley of the Leader or Lauder, a
river in Berwickshire. *Yarrow :* a stream in Selkirkshire.

Draws many a tear frae true love's e'e,
  When other maids are sleeping.

Yestreen I made my bed fu' braid,
  The nicht I'll mak' it narrow;
For, a' the live-lang winter nicht,
  I lie twinn'd o' my marrow.

O came ye by yon water side?
  Pou'd you the rose or lilie?
Or cam' ye by yon meadow green?
  Or saw ye my sweet Willie?"

She sought him up, she sought him doun,
  She sought the braid and narrow;
Syne, in the cleaving o' a craig,
  She found him drowned in Yarrow.

XXIII.

WALY, WALY.

O waly, waly up yon bank,
  And waly, waly doun yon brae,
And waly, waly by yon burn-side,
  Where I and my love wont to gae!
O waly, waly, but love is bonny
  A little while when it is new;
But when 'tis auld, it waxes cauld,
  And wears away like morning dew.

I lean'd my back unto an aik,
  I thought it was a trusty tree;

But first it bowed, and then it brak';
　And sae did my fause love to me.
O wherefore need I busk my head,
　Or wherefore need I kame my hair?
Sin my fause love has me forsook,
　And says he'll never love me mair.

Now Arthur's Seat shall be my bed,
　The sheets shall ne'er be press'd by me,
Saint Anton's Well shall be my drink,
　Since my true love's forsaken me.
Mart'mas wind, when wilt thou blaw,
　And shake the green leaves aff the tree?
O, gentle death, when wilt thou come
　And tak a life that wearies me?

'Tis not the frost that freezes fell,
　Nor blawing snaw's inclemencie;
'Tis not sic cauld that makes me cry:
　But my love's heart's grown cauld to me.
When we came in by Glasgow toun,
　We were a comely sicht to see;
My love was clad in velvet black,
　And I mysel' in cramasie.

But had I wist, before I kiss'd,
　That love had been sae ill to win,
I'd lock'd my heart in a case of gold,
　And pinn'd it wi' a siller pin.
Oh, oh! if my young babe were born,
　And set upon the nurse's knee,
And I mysel' were dead and gane,
　For a maid again I'll never be.

XXIV.

THE BRAES OF YARROW.

John Logan.—Born 1748; Died, 1788.

Thy braes were bonnie, Yarrow stream,
　When first on them I met my lover;
Thy braes how dreary, Yarrow stream,
　When now thy waves his body cover!
For ever now, O Yarrow stream!
　Thou art to me a stream of sorrow;
For never on thy banks shall I
　Behold my love, the flower of Yarrow.

He promised me a milk-white steed,
　To bear me to his father's bowers;
He promised me a little page,
　To squire me to his father's towers;
He promised me a wedding-ring;
　The wedding day was fixed to-morrow;
Now he is wedded to his grave,
　Alas, his watery grave, in Yarrow!

Sweet were his words when last we met;
　My passion I as freely told him;
Clasp'd in his arms, I never thought
　That I should never more behold him!
Scarce was he gone, I saw his ghost;
　It vanish'd with a shriek of sorrow;
Thrice did the water-wraith ascend,
　And gave a doleful groan through Yarrow.

His mother from the window looked,
　With all the longing of a mother;

His little sister, weeping, walked
  The greenwood path to meet her brother.
They sought him east, they sought him west.
  They sought him all the forest thorough;
They only saw the cloud of night,
  They only heard the roar of Yarrow!

No longer from thy window look;
  Thou hast no son, thou tender mother!
No longer walk, thou lovely maid;
  Alas, thou hast no more a brother!
No longer seek him east or west,
  And search no more the forest thorough!
For, wandering in the night so dark,
  He fell a lifeless corpse in Yarrow.

The tear shall never leave my cheek;
  No other youth shall be my marrow:
I'll seek thy body in the stream,
  And then with thee I'll sleep in Yarrow.
The tear did never leave her cheek;
  No other youth became her marrow;
She found his body in the stream,
  And now with him she sleeps in Yarrow.

XXV.

THE LAD THAT'S FAR AWA'.

R. Burns.

O how can I be blythe and glad,
  Or how can I gang brisk and braw,

When the bonnie lad that I lo'e best
  Is o'er the hills and far awa'?

It's no the frosty winter wind,
  It's no the driving drift and snaw;
But aye the tear comes in my e'e
  To think on him that's far awa'.

My father pat me frae his door,
  My friends they ha'e disown'd me a';
But there is ane will take my part,
  The bonnie lad that's far awa'.

A pair of gloves he bought to me,
  And silken snoods he ga'e me twa;
And I will wear them for his sake,
  The bonnie lad that's far awa'.

The weary winter soon will pass,
  And spring will cleed the birken shaw;
And my sweet babie will be born,
  And he'll be hame that's far awa'.

XXVI.

LEADER HAUGHS AND YARROW.

Minstrel Burne.

When Phœbus bright the azure skies
  With golden rays enlight'neth,
He makes all nature's beauties rise,
  Herbs, trees, and flowers he quick'neth:
Amongst all those he makes his choice,

And with delight goes thorow,
With radiant beams, the silver streams
    O'er Leader Haughs and Yarrow.

When Aries the day and night
    In equal length divideth,
And frosty Saturn takes his flight,
    Nae langer he abideth;
Then Flora queen, with mantle green,
    Casts off her former sorrow,
And vows to dwell with Ceres' sel',
    In Leader Haughs and Yarrow.

Pan, playing on his aiten reed,
    And shepherds, him attending,
Do here resort, their flocks to feed,
    The hills and haughs commending;
With cur and kent, upon the bent,
    Sing to the sun, good-morrow,
And swear nae fields mair pleasures yields
    Than Leader Haughs and Yarrow.

A house there stands on Leader side,
    Surmounting my descriving,
With rooms sae rare, and windows fair,
    Like Dædalus' contriving:
Men passing by do often cry,
    In sooth it hath nae marrow;
It stands as sweet on Leader side
    As Newark does on Yarrow.

A mile below, wha lists to ride,
    Will hear the mavis singing;
Into Saint Leonard's banks she'll bide,

Sweet birks her head owerhinging.
The lint-white loud, and gowdspink* proud,
  With tuneful throats and narrow,
Into Saint Leonard's banks they sing,
  As sweetly as in Yarrow.

The lapwing lilteth ower the lea,
  With nimble wing she sporteth;
But vows she'll flee far from the tree
  Where Philomel resorteth:
By break of day the lark can say,
  I'll bid you a good-morrow,
I'll streek my wing, and, mounting, sing
  O'er Leader Haughs and Yarrow.

Park, Wanton-wa's, and Wooden-cleugh,
  The East and Wester Mainses,
The wood of Lauder's fair eneugh,
  The corns are good in Blainshes,
Where aits are fine, and sold by kind,
  That if ye search all thorough
Mearns, Buchan, Mar, nane better are
  Than Leader Haughs and Yarrow.

In Burnmill Bog and Whiteslade Shaws,
  The fearful hare she haunteth;
Brig-haugh and Braidwoodshiel she knaws,
  And Chapel-wood frequenteth:
Yet when she irks to Kaidslie Birks,
  She rins and sighs for sorrow,

* We have here used the word *gowdspink*, instead of
Progne, as being more in keeping with the simplicity of
the song; and, at any rate, Progne is inappropriate, as
the swallow never sings.—ED.

C

That she should leave sweet Leader Haughs,
  And cannot win to Yarrow.

What sweeter music wad ye hear
  Than hounds and beagles crying?
The startled hare rins hard with fear,
  Upon her speed relying:
But yet her strength it fails at length;
  Nae bielding can she borrow,
In Sorrel's fields, Clackmae, or Hags;
  And sighs to be on Yarrow.

For Rockwood, Ringwood, Spotty, Shag,
  With sight and scent pursue her;
Till, ah, her pith begins to flag;
  Nae cunning can rescue her:
Ower dub and dyke, ower seugh and syke,
  She'll rin the fields all thorough,
Till, failed, she fa's on Leader Haughs,
  And bids fareweel to Yarrow.

Sing Erslington and Cowdenknowes,
  Where Homes had ance commanding;
And Drygrange, with the milk-white yowes,
  'Twixt Tweed and Leader standing.
The bird that flees through Reedpath trees
  And Gledswood banks ilk morrow,
May chaunt and sing sweet Leader Haughs
  And bonnie Howms of Yarrow.

But Minstrel Burne cannot assuage
  His grief, while life endureth,
To see the changes of this age,
  That fleeting time procureth:

For many a place stands in hard case,
　　Where blythe folk kend nae sorrow,
With Homes that dwelt on Leader-side,
　　And Scotts that dwelt on Yarrow.

This very long song, in which, however, the old violer (or "minstrel," as he styles himself) does little more than lovingly repeat the names of the places dear to him, is so full of melody and of tender mournful simplicity that it has for a long time, some say two centuries, been a favourite with the Scotch people; and on this account we have inserted it here. Of the author, nothing whatever is known, except the name which his song gives him, " Minstrel Burne."

XXVII.

AULD ROBIN GRAY.

Lady Anne Lindsay, afterwards Barnard.
Born 1750; Died 1825.

When the sheep are in the fauld, and the kye at
　　　hame,
And a' the warld to sleep are gane;
The waes o' my heart fa' in showers frae my e'e,
When my gudeman lies sound by me.

Young Jamie lo'ed me weel, and sought me for
　　　his bride,
But saving a crown he had naething else beside;
To make that crown a pound, my Jamie gaed to
　　　sea;
And the crown and the pound were baith for
　　　me.

He hadna been awa' a week but only twa,
When my mother she fell sick, and the cow was
       stown awa' ;
My father brak' his arm, and my Jamie at the
       sea,
And auld Robin Gray cam a-courting me.

My father couldna work, and my mother couldna
       spin,
I toil'd day and night, but their bread I couldna
       win ;
Auld Rob maintain'd them baith, and wi' tears
       in his e'e,
Said, Jenny, for their sakes, O marry me.

My heart it said nay, I look'd for Jamie back ;
But the wind it blew high, and the ship it was a
       wreck :
The ship it was a wreck, why didna Jamie dee?
And why do I live to say, Wae's me ?

My father argued sair, though my mother didna
       speak,
She look'd in my face till my heart was like to
       break ;
So they gi'ed him my hand, though my heart was
       at the sea,
And auld Robin Gray is gudeman to me.

I hadna' been a wife a week but only four,
When mournfu' as I sat on the stane at the door,
I saw my Jamie's wraith, for I couldna think it he,
Till he said, I'm come back for to marry thee.

O sair did we greet, and muckle did we say,
We took but ae kiss, and we tore ourselves away ;
I wish I were dead ! but I'm no like to dee ;
And why do I live to say, Wae's me ?

I gang like a ghaist, and I carena to spin ;
I darena think on Jamie, for that would be a sin ;
But I'll do my best a gude wife to be,
For auld Robin Gray is kind to me.

XXVIII.

THE FLOWERS OF THE FOREST.

Jane Elliot.—Born 1727 ; Died 1805.

I've heard them lilting, at our ewe-milking,
Lasses a-lilting, before the dawn of day ;
But now they are moaning, on ilka green loaning ;
The Flowers of the Forest are a' wede away.

At bughts in the morning nae blythe lads are
     scorning ;
The lasses are lanely, and dowie, and wae ;
Nae daffing, nae gabbing, but sighing and sabbing.
Ilk ane lifts her leglin, and hies her away.

In hairst, at the shearing, nae youths now are
     jeering,
The bandsters are lyart, and runkled and gray ;
At fair or at preaching, nae wooing, nae fleech
     ing—
The Flowers of the Forest are a' wede away.

* Ettrick Forest ; it comprehends a great part of the
county of Selkirk.

At e'en, in the gloaming, nae swankies are roam-
　　　ing
'Bout stacks wi' the lasses at bogle to play;
But ilk ane sits eerie, lamenting her dearie—
The Flowers of the Forest are a' wede away.

Dool and wae for the order sent our lads to the
　　　Border !
The English, for ance, by guile wan the day;
The Flowers of the Forest, that fought aye the
　　　foremost,
The prime of our land, lie cauld in the clay.

We'll hear nae mair lilting at our ewe-milking,
Women and bairns are heartless and wae ;
Sighing and moaning on ilka green loaning,
The Flowers of the Forest are a' wede away.

XXIX.

THE FLOWERS OF THE FOREST.

Alison Rutherford, afterwards Mrs. Cockburn.
Died 1794; Aged about 80.

I've seen the smiling of fortune beguiling,
I've felt all its favours, and found its decay ;
Sweet was its blessing, and kind its caressing,
But now it is fled—it is fled far away.

I've seen the Forest adorned of the foremost,
With flowers of the fairest, most pleasant and gay;
Full sweet was their blooming, their scent the
　　　air perfuming,
But now they are withered, and a' wede away.

I've seen the morning, with gold the hills adorn-
    ing,
And the loud tempest roaring, before the parting
    day ;
I've seen Tweed's silver streams, glittering in the
    sunny beams,
Turn drumly and dark, as they rolled on their
    way.

O fickle Fortune ! why this cruel sporting?
Why thus perplex us, poor sons of a day?
Thy frowns cannot fear me, thy smiles cannot
    cheer me,
For the Flowers of the Forest are a' wede away.

XXX.

THE BONNY EARL OF MURRAY.

Ye highlands and ye lawlands,
    Oh ! where ha'e ye been ?
They ha'e slain the Earl of Murray,
    And ha'e laid him on the green.

Now wae be to thee Huntley !
    And wherefore did you sae ?
I bade you bring him wi' you,
    But forbade you him to slay.

He was a braw gallant ;
    And he rade at the ring ;
And the bonny Earl of Murray,
    Oh ! he might ha' been a king.

He was a braw gallant,
  And he play'd at the ba';
And the bonny Earl of Murray
  Was the flower amang them a'.

He was a braw gallant,
  And he play'd at the glove;
And the bonny Earl of Murray,
  Oh! he was the queen's love.

Oh! lang will his lady
  Look ow'r the castle downe,
Ere she see the Earl of Murray
  Cum sounding throw the towne.

XXXI.

GILDEROY.

Gilderoy was a bonnie boy
  Had roses tull his shoon;
His stockings were of silken soy,
  Wi' gartars hanging downe;
It was I ween a comely sicht,
  To see sae trim a boy;
He was my joy and heart's delicht,
  My handsome Gilderoy.

O sic twa charming een he had,
  A breath as sweet's a rose;
He never wore a Highland plaid,
  But costly silken clothes:
He gain'd the love of ladies gay,
  Nane e'er to him was coy:

Ah, wae is me ! I mourn the day,
  For my dear Gilderoy.

For Gilderoy, that love of mine,
  Gude faith, I freely bought
A wedding sark of holland fine,
  Wi' silken flowers wrought;
And he gied me a wedding ring,
  Which I received wi' joy :
Nae lad nor lassie e'er could sing
  Like me and Gilderoy.

Oh, that he still had been content
  Wi' me to lead his life !
But, ah, his manfu' heart was bent
  To stir in feats of strife ;
And he in many a venturous deed
  His courage bauld wad try,
And now this gars my heart to bleed
  For my dear Gilderoy.

And when of me his leave he took,
  The tears they wat mine e'e ;
I gave to him a parting look,
  " My benison gang wi' thee !
God speed thee weel, mine ain dear heart
  For gane is all my joy ;
My heart is rent, sith we maun part,
  My handsome Gilderoy."

My Gilderoy, baith far and near,
  Was fear'd in ilka toun,
And bauldly bare away the gear
  Of mony a Lawland loun :

Nane e'er durst meet him man to man,
    He was sae brave a boy;
At length wi' numbers he was ta'en,
    My handsome Gilderoy.

Wae worth the loun that made the laws
    To hang a man for gear!
To reave of life for ox or ass,
    For sheep, or horse, or mear!
Had not the laws been made so strick,
    I ne'er had lost my joy,
Wi' sorrow ne'er had wat my cheik
    For my dear Gilderoy.

Gif Gilderoy had done amiss,
    He micht have banish'd been;
Ah! what sair cruelty is this,
    To hang sic handsome men!
To hang the flower o' Scottish land,
    Sae sweet and fair a boy!
Nae lady had sae white a hand
    As thou, my Gilderoy.

Of Gilderoy sae fear'd they were,
    They bound him meikle strong;
Tull Edinburgh they led him there,
    And on a gallows hung;
They hung him high abune the rest,
    He was sae trim a boy;
There died the youth whom I lo'ed best,
    My handsome Gilderoy.

Gilderoy was a celebrated Highland freebooter, who,
with five of his comrades, was executed in Edinburgh in

1638. This ballad is a great favourite in Scotland; and
is sung to what Miss Ferrier calls the queen of all the
Scotch tunes. Lady Wardlaw (1677 to 1727) altered the
words of the older ballad, which were supposed to be
somewhat indelicate; we have given her version *minus*
four stanzas.

XXXII.

THE LOW LANDS OF HOLLAND.

My love has built a bonnie ship, and set her on
    the sea,
With seven-score good mariners to bear her
    companie,
There's three-score is sunk, and three-score dead
    at sea,
And the low lands of Holland hae twin'd my
    love and me.

My love he built anither ship, and set her on
    the main,
And nane but twenty mariners for to bring her
    hame,
But the weary wind began to rise, and the sea
    began to rout,
My love then and his bonnie ship turn'd wither-
    shins about.

There shall neither coif come on my head, nor
    comb come in my hair,
There shall neither coal nor candle light shine
    in my bower mair;
Nor will I love anither ane until the day I dee;
For I never loved a love but ane, and he's
    drown'd in the sea.

Oh haud your tongue, my daughter dear, be still
      and be content;
There are mair lads in Galloway, ye needna sair
      lament.
Oh ! there is nane in Galloway, there's nane at
      a' for me ;
For I never loved a love but ane, and he's
      drown'd in the sea.

XXXIII.

BARBARA ALLAN.

It was in and about the Martinmas time,
  When the green leaves were a-fallin',
That Sir John Græme in the west countrie,
  Fell in love wi' Barbara Allan.

He sent his man down through the town,
  To the place where she was dwallin',
O, haste and come to my master dear,
  Gin ye be Barbara Allan.

O, hooly, hooly, rase she up
  To the place where he was lying,
And when she drew the curtain by,
  "Young man, I think ye're dying."

"It's oh, I'm sick, I'm very very sick,
  And it's a' for Barbara Allan."
"O, the better for me ye'se never be,
  Though your heart's blude were a-spillin'."

"Oh, dinna you mind, young man," said she,
　"When ye was in the tavern a-drinkin',
That ye made the healths gae round and round
　And slichtit Barbara Allan?"

He turned his face unto the wall,
　And death was with him dealin':
"Adieu, adieu, my dear friends a',
　And be kind to Barbara Allan."

Then slowly, slowly rase she up,
　And slowly, slowly left him,
And sighin', said, she could not stay,
　Since death of life had reft him.

She hadna gane a mile but twa,
　When she heard the deid-bell ringin';
And every jow that the deid-bell gied,
　It cried, woe to Barbara Allan.

"Oh, mother, mother, mak' my bed,
　And mak' it saft and narrow;
Since my love died for me to-day,
　I'll die for him to-morrow."

We have heard it remarked of this ballad, that
"there is not a more gratuitous tragedy on record."

XXXIV.

WARENA MY HEART LICHT I WAD DEE.

Lady Grisell Home, afterwards Baillie.
Born 1665 ; Died 1746.

There ance was a May, and she lo'ed na men,
She biggit her bonnie bower doun in yon glen ;

But now she cries, Dool ! and awell-a-day !
Come down the green gate, and come here away.

When bonnie young Johnnie cam' o'er the sea,
He said he saw naething sae lovely as me ;
He hecht me rings and monie braw things
And were na my heart licht I wad dee.

He had a wee titty that lo'ed na me,
Because I was twice as bonnie as she ;
She rais'd such a pother 'twixt him and his mother,
That were na my heart licht I wad dee.

The day it was set, and the bridal to be,
The wife took a dwam, and lay down to dee ;
She man'd and she graned, out of dolour and pain,
Till he vow'd he never wad see me again.

His kin was for ane of a higher degree,
Said, What had he to do with the like of me ?
Albeit I was bonnie, I was na for Johnnie :
And were na my heart licht I wad dee.

They said I had neither cow nor calf,
Nor dribbles of drink rins through the draff,
Nor pickles of meal rins through the mill-e'e ;
And were na my heart licht I wad dee.

His titty she was baith wylie and slee,
She spied me as I cam' ower the lea ;
And then she ran in, and made a loud din,
Believe your ain een, an ye trow no me.

His bonnet stood aye fu' round on his brow ;
His auld ane look'd aye as weel as some's new ;

But now he lets 't wear ony gate it will hing,
And casts himself dowie upon the corn-bing.

And now he gaes daundring about the dykes.
And a' he dow do is to hund the tykes :
The live-lang nicht he ne'er steeks his e'e ;
And were na my heart licht I wad dee.

Were I young for thee, as I ha'e been,
We should ha'e been gallopin' down on yon green.
And linkin' it on the lily-white lea ;
And wow ! gin I were but young for thee !

XXXV.

THE POOR AND HONEST SODGER.

R. Burns.

When wild war's deadly blast was blawn,
  And gentle peace returning,
Wi' mony a sweet babe fatherless,
  And mony a widow mourning ;
I left the lines and tented field,
  Where lang I'd been I lodger,
My humble knapsack a' my wealth,
  A poor but honest sodger.

A leal light heart beat in my breast,
  My hands unstain'd wi' plunder ;
And for fair Scotia hame again,
  I cheery on did wander.
I thought upon the banks o' Coil,
  I thought upon my Nancy ;

I thought upon the witching smile,
　That caught my youthful fancy.

At length I reach'd the bonnie glen,
　Where early life I sported ;
I pass'd the mill and trysting thorn,
　Where Nancy oft I courted.
Wha spied I but my ain dear maid,
　Down by her mother's dwelling ?
And turned me round to hide the flood
　That in my e'e was swelling.

Wi' alter'd voice, quoth I, Sweet lass,
　Sweet as yon hawthorn's blossom,
O ! happy, happy may he be,
　That's dearest to thy bosom.
My purse is light, I've far to gang,
　And fain would be thy lodger,
I've served my king and country lang ;
　Take pity on a sodger.

Sae wistfully she gazed on me,
　And lovelier grew than ever ;
Quoth she, A sodger ance I lo'ed,
　Forget him shall I never.
Our humble cot and hamely fare,
　Ye freely shall partake o't ;
That gallant badge, the dear cockade,
　Ye're welcome for the sake o't.

She gazed—she redden'd like a rose—
　Syne pale as ony lily ;
She sank within my arms, and cried,
　Art thou my ain dear Willie ?

By Him, who made yon sun and sky,
   By whom true love's regarded,
I am the man ! and thus may still
   True lovers be rewarded.

The wars are o'er, and I'm come hame,
   And find thee still true-hearted ;
Though poor in gear, we're rich in love,
   And mair we'se ne'er be parted.
Quoth she, My grandsire left me gowd,
   A mailin' plenish'd fairly ;
Then come, my faithfu' sodger lad,
   Thou'rt welcome to it dearly !

For gold the merchant ploughs the main,
   The farmer ploughs the manor ;
But glory is the sodger's prize,
   The sodger's wealth is honour ;
The brave poor sodger ne'er despise,
   Nor count him as a stranger ;
Remember he's his country's stay,
   In day and hour of danger.

XXXVI.

ANNAN'S WINDING STREAM.

Stewart Lewis.—Died 1818.

On Annan's banks, in life's gay morn,
   I tuned my wood-notes wild ;

D

I sang of flocks and flow'ry plains,
    Like nature's simple child.
Some talked of wealth—I heard of fame,
    But thought 'twas all a dream ;
For dear I loved a village maid
    By Annan's winding stream.

The dew-bespangled blushing rose,
    The garden's joy and pride,
Was ne'er so fragrant nor so fair,
    As she I wished my bride.
The sparkling radiance of her eye,
    Was bright as Phœbus' beam ;
Each grace adorn'd my village maid
    By Annan's winding stream.

But war's shrill clarion fiercely blew ;
    The sound alarmed my ear ;
My country's wrongs call'd for redress ;
    Could I my aid forbear?
No ;—soon, in warlike garb array'd,
    With arms that bright did gleam,
I sigh'd, and left my village maid
    By Annan's winding stream.

Perhaps blest peace may soon return,
    With all her smiling train ;
For Britain's conquests still proclaim
    Her sovereign of the main.
With joy I'd quit the gay parade,
    And canvass-cover'd plain ;
And haste to clasp my village maid
    By Annan's winding stream.

XXXVII.

DONOCHT-HEAD.

Keen blaws the wind o'er Donocht-Head,
   The snaw drives snelly through the dale,
The gaberlunzie tirls my sneck,
   And, shiv'ring, tells his waefu' tale :
'Cauld is the night, O let me in,
   And dinna let your Minstrel fa',
And dinna let his winding-sheet
   Be naething but a wreath o' snaw.

Full ninety winters ha'e I seen,
   And piped whare gorcocks whirring flew
And mony a day ye've danc'd, I ween,
   To lilts which frae my drone I blew'.—
My Eppie wak'd, and soon she cried,
   'Get up, gudeman, and let him in ;
For weel ye ken the winter night
   Was short when he began his din.'

My Eppie's voice, O wow ! it's sweet !
   E'en though she bans and scolds a wee ;
But when it's tuned to sorrow's tale
   O, haith, it's doubly dear to me !

'Come in, auld carle ! I'll steer my fire,
   And mak' it bleeze a bonnie flame ;
Your blude is thin, ye've tint the gate,
   Ye should nae stray sae far frae hame.'
'Nae hame ha'e I,' the Minstrel said,
   'Sad party strife o'erturn'd my ha' ;

And, weeping, at the eve o' life
    I wander through a wreath o' snaw.'

"*Donnocht-Head* is not mine; I would give ten pounds it were."—*Burns.*

XXXVIII.

MARY MORISON.

R. Burns.

O Mary, at thy window be,
    It is the wish'd, the trysted hour!
Those smiles and glances let me see
    That make the miser's treasure poor.
How blithely wad I bide the stoure,
    A weary slave frae sun to sun,
Could I the rich reward secure,
    The lovely Mary Morison.

Yestreen, when to the trembling string
    The dance gaed through the lichtit ha',
To thee my fancy took its wing—
    I sat, but neither heard nor saw.
Though this was fair, and that was braw,
    And yon the toast of a' the town,
I sigh'd, and said amang them a',
    "Ye are na Mary Morison."

O Mary, canst thou wreck his peace,
    Wha for thy sake wad gladly die?
Or canst thou break that heart of his,
    Whase only faut is loving thee?

If love for love thou wilt na gie,
  At least be pity to me shown ;
A thought ungentle canna be
  The thought o' Mary Morison.

Hazlitt considers this one of the best songs which Burns has written.

XXXIX.

AFTON WATER.

R. Burns.

Flow gently, sweet Afton, among thy green braes,
Flow gently, I'll sing thee a song in thy praise ;
My Mary's asleep by thy murmuring stream ;
Flow gently, sweet Afton, disturb not her dream.

Thou stock-dove, whose echo resounds through
    the glen,
Ye wild whistling blackbirds, in yon thorny den,
Thou green-crested lap-wing, thy screaming for-
    bear,
I charge you, disturb not my slumbering fair.

How lofty, sweet Afton, thy neighbouring hills,
Far mark'd with the courses of clear, winding
    rills ;
There daily I wander, as noon rises high,
My flocks and my Mary's sweet cot in my eye.

How pleasant thy banks and green valleys below,
Where wild in the woodlands the primroses blow ;
There oft, as mild evening creeps over the lea,
The sweet-scented birk shades my Mary and me.

Thy crystal stream, Afton, how lovely it glides,
And winds by the cot where my Mary resides,
How wanton thy waters her snowy feet lave,
As gathering sweet flow'rets, she stems thy clear
   wave.

Flow gently, sweet Afton, among thy green braes,
Flow gently, sweet river, the theme of my lays;
My Mary's asleep by thy murmuring stream,
Flow gently, sweet Afton, disturb not her dream.

XL.

HIGHLAND MARY.

R. Burns.

Ye banks and braes and streams around
  The castle o' Montgomery,
Green be your woods, and fair your flowers,
  Your waters never drumlie!
There simmer first unfaulds her robes,
  And there the langest tarry;
For there I took the last fareweel
 O' my sweet Highland Mary.

How sweetly bloom'd the gay green birk,
  How rich the hawthorn's blossom,
As underneath their fragrant shade,
  I clasp'd her to my bosom!
The golden hours, on angel wings,
  Flew o'er me and my dearie;
For dear to me as light and life
  Was my sweet Highland Mary.

Wi' monie a vow, and lock'd embrace,
　Our parting was fu' tender;
And pledging aft to meet again,
　We tore ourselves asunder:
But oh! fell death's untimely frost,
　That nipt my flower sae early!—
Now green's the sod, and cauld's the clay,
　That wraps my Highland Mary!

O pale, pale now those rosy lips
　I aft hae kiss'd sae fondly!
And clos'd for aye the sparkling glance,
　That dwelt on me sae kindly;
And mouldering now in silent dust,
　That heart that lo'ed me dearly—
But still within my bosom's core
　Shall live my Highland Mary.

"The subject of this song is one of the most interesting passages of my youthful days, and I own that I
should be much flattered to see the verses set to an air
which would ensure celebrity."—*Burns.*

XLI.

TO MARY IN HEAVEN.

R. Burns.

Thou ling'ring star, with less'ning ray,
　That lov'st to greet the early morn,
Again thou usher'st in the day,
　My Mary from my soul was torn.
Oh, Mary, dear departed shade!
　Where is thy place of blissful rest?
See'st thou thy lover lowly laid?
　Hear'st thou the groans that rend his breast?

That sacred hour can I forget,
  Can I forget the hallow'd grove,
Where, by the winding Ayr, we met,
  To live one day of parting love?
Eternity can not efface
  Those records dear of transports past,
Thy image at our last embrace;
  Ah! little thought we 'twas our last!

Ayr, gurgling, kiss'd his pebbled shore,
  O'erhung with wild woods, thick'ning green;
The fragrant birch, and hawthorn hoar,
  Twined am'rous round the raptur'd scene.
The flow'rs sprang wanton to be prest,
  The birds sang love on every spray;
Till too, too soon, the glowing west
  Proclaim'd the speed of winged day.

Still o'er these scenes my mem'ry wakes,
  And fondly broods with miser care;
Time but the impression stronger makes,
  As streams their channels deeper wear.
My Mary, dear departed shade!
  Where is thy place of blissful rest?
See'st thou thy lover lowly laid?
  Hear'st thou the groans that rend his breast?

XLII.

MARY'S DREAM.

John Lowe.—Born 1750; Died 1798.

The moon had climb'd the highest hill,
  Which rises o'er the source of Dee,

And from the eastern summit shed
  Her silver light on tower and tree;
When Mary laid her down to sleep,
  Her thoughts on Sandy far at sea;
When soft and low, a voice was heard,
  Saying, " Mary, weep no more for me !"

She from her pillow gently raised
  Her head, to ask who there might be;
She saw young Sandy shivering stand,
  With visage pale, and hollow e'e.
" O Mary dear, cold is my clay;
  It lies beneath a stormy sea.
Far, far from thee, I sleep in death,
  So, Mary, weep no more for me !

Three stormy nights and stormy days,
  We tossed upon the raging main;
And long we strove our bark to save,
  But all our striving was in vain.
Even then, when horror chilled my blood,
  My heart was filled with love for thee:
The storm is past, and I at rest;
  So, Mary, weep no more for me !

O maiden dear, thyself prepare;
  We soon shall meet upon that shore,
Where love is free from doubt and care,
  And thou and I shall part no more !"
Loud crowed the cock, the shadow fled:
  No more of Sandy could she see.
But soft the passing spirit said,
  " Sweet Mary, weep no more for me !"

XLIII.

James Beattie.—Born 1735; Died 1803.

On a rock by seas surrounded,
    Distant far from sight of shore,
When the shipwreck'd wretch, confounded,
    Hears the bellowing tempest roar,
Hopes of life do then forsake him,
    In this last deplor'd extreme;
When, lo! his own loud shrieks awake him,
    And he finds it all a dream.

XLIV.

LORD ULLIN'S DAUGHTER.

Thomas Campbell.—Born 1777; Died 1844.

A chieftain to the Highlands bound,
    Cries, 'Boatman, do not tarry!
And I'll give thee a silver pound
    To row us o'er the ferry!'—

'Now who be ye would cross Lochgyle,
    This dark and stormy water?'
'O I'm the chief of Ulva's Isle,
    And this Lord Ullin's daughter.

'And fast before her father's men
    Three days we've fled together,
For should he find us in the glen
    My blood would stain the heather.

'His horsemen hard behind us ride—
　　Should they our steps discover,
Then who will cheer my bonny bride
　　When they have slain her lover?'—

Out spoke the hardy Highland wight,
　　'I'll go, my chief, I'm ready:
It is not for your silver bright,
　　But for your winsome lady:—

'And by my word! the bonny bird
　　In danger shall not tarry;
So though the waves are raging white,
　　I'll row you o'er the ferry.'

By this the storm grew loud apace,
　　The water-wraith was shrieking;
And in the scowl of heaven each face
　　Grew dark as they were speaking.

But still as wilder blew the wind
　　And as the night grew drearer,
Adown the glen rode armèd men,
　　Their trampling sounded nearer.

'O haste thee, haste!' the lady cries,
　　'Though tempests round us gather;
I'll meet the raging of the skies,
　　But not an angry father.'

The boat has left a stormy land,
　　A stormy sea before her,—
When O! too strong for human hand,
　　The tempest gather'd o'er her.

And still they row'd against the roar
  Of waters fast prevailing;
Lord Ullin reach'd that fatal shore,—
  His wrath was changed to wailing.

For sore dismayed, through storm and shade,
  He did his child discover:—
One lovely hand she stretched for aid,
  And one was round her lover.

'Come back! come back!' he cried in grief,
  'Across this stormy water:
And I'll forgive your Highland chief,
  My daughter!—O my daughter!'

'Twas vain: the loud waves lash'd the shore,
  Return or aid preventing:
The waters wild went o'er his child,
  And he was left lamenting.

XLV.

MY DEARIE, IF THOU DEE.

R. Crawford.

Love never more shall give me pain,
  My fancy's fixed on thee;
Nor ever maid my heart shall gain,
  My Peggie, if thou dee.
Thy beauties did such pleasure give,
  Thy love's so true to me;
Without thee I shall never live,
  My dearie, if thou dee.

If fate shall tear thee from my breast,
   How shall I lonely stray !
In dreary dreams the night I'll waste,
   In sighs the silent day.
I ne'er can so much virtue find,
   Nor such perfection see :
Then I'll renounce all womankind,
   My Peggie, after thee.

No new-blown beauty fires my heart,
   With Cupid's raving rage ;
But thine, which can such sweets impart,
   Must all the world engage.
'Twas this that like the morning sun,
   Gave joy and life to me ;
And, when its destin'd day is done,
   With Peggie let me dee.

Ye powers that smile on virtuous love,
   And in such pleasure share,
Ye who its faithful flames approve,
   With pity view the fair :
Restore my Peggie's wonted charms,
   Those charms so dear to me ;
Oh, never rob them from my arms ;
   I'm lost if Peggie dee.

XLVI.

FAREWELL TO LOCHABER.

Allan Ramsay.

Farewell to Lochaber, and farewell, my Jean,
Where heartsome with thee I've mony a day been ;

For Lochaber no more, Lochaber no more,
We'll maybe return to Lochaber no more.
These tears that I shed, they're a' for my dear,
And no for the dangers attending on weir;
Though borne on rough seas to a far bloody
    shore,
Maybe to return to Lochaber no more !

Though hurricanes rise, and rise every wind,
They'll ne'er make a tempest like that in my mind;
Though loudest of thunders on louder waves roar,
That's naething like leaving my love on the shore.
To leave thee behind me my heart is sair pain'd,
But by ease that's inglorious no fame can be
    gain'd :
And beauty and love's the reward of the brave ;
And I maun deserve it before I can crave.

Then glory, my Jeany, maun plead my excuse,
Since honour commands me, how can I refuse?
Without it I ne'er can have merit for thee ;
And wanting thy favour I'd better not be.
I go then, my lass, to win honour and fame ;
And if I should luck to come gloriously hame,
I'll bring thee a heart with love running o'er,
And then I'll leave thee and Lochaber no more.

XLVII.

THE WIDOW'S LAMENT.

Thomas Smibert.

Afore the Lammas tide
   Had dun'd the birken tree,

In a' our water-side
  Nae wife was blest like me;
A kind gudeman, and twa
  Sweet bairns were round me here,
But they're a' ta'en awa'
  Sin' the fa' o' the year.

Sair trouble cam' our gate,
  And made me, when it cam',
A bird without a mate,
  A ewe without a lamb.
Our hay was yet to maw,
  And our corn was to shear,
When they a' dwined awa'
  In the fa' o' the year.

I downa look a-field,
  For aye I trow I see,
The form that was a bield
  To my wee bairns and me;
But wind, and weet, and snaw,
  They never mair can fear,
Sin' they a' got the ca'
  In the fa' o' the year.

Aft on the hill at e'ens
  I see him mang the ferns,
The lover o' my teens,
  The father o' my bairns:
For there his plaid I saw
  As gloaming aye drew near—
But my a's now awa'
  Sin' the fa' o' the year.

Our bonnie rigs theirsel',
    Reca' my waes to mind,
Our puir dumb beasties tell
    O' a' that I have tined ;
For whae our wheat will saw,
    And whae our sheep will shear,
Sin' my a' gaed awa'
    In the fa' o' the year?

My heart is growing cauld,
    And will be caulder still ;
And sair, sair in the fauld
    Will be the winter's chill ;
For peats were yet to ca',
    Our sheep they were to smear,
When my a' dwined awa'
    In the fa' o' the year.

I ettle whiles to spin,
    But wee, wee patterin' feet
Come rinnin' out and in,
    And then I just maun greet :
I ken it's fancy a',
    And faster rows the tear,
That my a' dwined awa'
    In the fa' o' the year.

Be kind, O heav'n abune !
    To ane sae wae and lane,
An' tak' her hamewards sune,
    In pity o' her mane :
Long ere the March winds blaw,
    May she, far far frae here,
Meet them a' that's awa'
    Sin' the fa' o' the year.

XLVIII.

LOGAN BRAES.

John Mayne.—Born 1759; Died 1836.

By Logan's streams that rin sae deep
Fu' aft, wi' glee, I've herded sheep,
I've herded sheep, or gather'd slaes,
Wi' my dear lad, on Logan braes.
But wae's my heart ! thae days are gane,
And fu' o' grief I herd alane,
While my dear lad maun face his faes,
Far, far frae me and Logan braes.

Nae mair, at Logan kirk, will he,
Atween the preachings, meet wi' me—
Meet wi' me, or when it's mirk,
Convoy me hame frae Logan kirk.
I weel may sing thae days are gane—
Frae kirk and fair I come alane,
While my dear lad maun face his faes,
Far, far frae me and Logan braes !

At e'en, when hope amaist is gane,
I dander dowie and forlane,
Or sit beneath the trysting-tree,
Where first he spak o' love to me.
O ! cou'd I see thae days again,
My lover skaithless, and my ain ;
Rever'd by friends, and far frae faes,
We'd live in bliss on Logan braes.

Mayne was the author of the *Siller Gun*, a Poem describing the practice of shooting for a little silver gun,

which James VI. had presented to the town of Dumfries,
and which was, at stated intervals, for many years com-
peted for by the townspeople. The Poem is witty and
clever, in a rather unusual degree ; but the allusions being
chiefly local and personal, it is now to a great extent
forgotten.

XLIX.

THE BUSH ABOON TRAQUAIR.

Robert Crawford.

Hear me, ye nymphs, and ev'ry swain,
   I'll tell how Peggy grieves me ;
Tho' thus I languish and complain,
   Alas, she ne'er believes me.
My vows and sighs, like silent air,
   Unheeded never move her.
The bonny bush aboon Traquair,
   Was where I first did love her.

That day she smiled, and made me glad,
   No maid seem'd ever kinder,
I thought myself the luckiest lad,
   So sweetly there to find her.
I tried to soothe my am'rous flame,
   In words that I thought tender :
If more there pass'd, I'm not to blame
   I meant not to offend her.

Yet now she scornful flees the plain,
   The fields we then frequented ;
If e'er we meet, she shows disdain,
   She looks as ne'er acquainted.

The bonnie bush bloom'd fair in May,
   It's sweets I'll aye remember;
But now her frowns make it decay;
   It fades as in December.

Ye rural pow'rs who hear my strains,
   Why thus should Peggy grieve me?
Oh! make her partner in my pains;
   Then let her smiles relieve me.
If not, my love will turn despair,
   My passion no more tender,
I'll leave the bush aboon Traquair,
   To lonely wilds I'll wander.

The 'Bush aboon Traquair' was a plantation, of which,
we are told, only a "few solitary ragged trees" now
remain, close to Traquair House in Peebleshire.

L.

William Hamilton of Bangour.—Born 1704; Died 1754.

Ah the shepherd's mournful fate,
   When doom'd to love and doom'd to languish,
To bear the scornful fair one's hate,
   Nor dare disclose his anguish!
Yet eager looks, and dying sighs
   My secret soul discover,
While rapture, trembling through mine eyes,
   Reveals how much I love her.
The tender glance, the reddening cheek,
   O'erspread with rising blushes,
A thousand various ways they speak
   A thousand various wishes.

For, oh ! that form so heavenly fair,
　Those languid eyes so sweetly smiling,
That artless blush and modest air,
　So fatally beguiling,
Thy every look, and every grace,
　So charm, whene'er I view thee,
Till death o'ertake me in the chase
　Still will my hopes pursue thee.
Then, when my tedious hours are past,
　Be this last blessing given,
Low at thy feet to breathe my last,
　And die in sight of heaven.

Hamilton was one of the "ingenious young gentle-men" who contributed to Allan Ramsay's *Tea Table Mis-cellany.* His songs were at one time popular in Scot-land. He became involved in the rebellion of 1745; after lurking for some time in the Highlands, he escaped to France, where, after several years of exile, he died.

LI.

WHY HANGS THAT CLOUD.

William Hamilton of Bangour.

Why hangs that cloud upon thy brow,
That beauteous heav'n erewhile serene?
Whence do these storms and tempests flow,
Or what this gust of passion mean?
And must then mankind lose that light
Which in thine eyes was wont to shine,
And lie obscur'd in endless night,
For each poor silly speech of mine?

Dear child, how could I wrong thy name,
Since 'tis acknowledged on all hands,
That could ill tongues abuse thy fame,
Thy beauty would make large amends :
Or if I durst profanely try
Thy beauty's pow'rful charms t' upbraid,
Thy virtue well might give the lie,
Nor call thy beauty to its aid.

For Venus every heart t' ensnare,
With all her charms has deck'd thy face,
And Pallas, with unusual care,
Bids wisdom heighten every grace.
Who can the double pain endure?
Or who must not resign the field
To thee, celestial maid, secure
With Cupid's bow and Pallas' shield?

If then to thee such power is giv'n,
Let not a wretch in torment live,
But smile, and learn to copy Heav'n,
Since we must sin ere it forgive.
Yet pitying Heaven not only does
Forgive th' offender and the offence,
But even itself, appeas'd, bestows,
As the reward of penitence.

LII.

THOU ART GANE AWA'.

Sir Alexander Boswell, Bart.—Born 1775 ; Died 1822.

Thou art gane awa', thou art gane awa'
  Thou art gane awa' frae me, Mary !

Nor friends nor I could make thee stay,
    Thou has cheated them and me, Mary.
Until this hour I never thought
    That aught could alter thee, Mary;
Thou'rt still the mistress of my heart,
    Think what you will of me, Mary.

Whate'er he said or might pretend,
    Who stole that heart of thine, Mary,
True love, I'm sure, was ne'er his end,
    Or nae sic love as mine, Mary.
I spoke sincere, nor flattered much,
    Nae selfish thoughts in me, Mary;
Ambition, wealth, nor naething such;
    No, I loved only thee, Mary.

Though you've been false, yet while I live,
    I'll lo'e nae maid but thee, Mary;
Let friends forget, as I forgive,
    Thy wrongs to them and me, Mary:
So then, fareweel! of this be·sure,
    Since you've been false to me, Mary;
For all the world I'd not endure
    Half what I've done for thee, Mary.

Alexander Boswell (created a baronet in 1821), the author of this and one or two other songs, was the eldest son of Johnson's Boswell. He was connected with a violent Tory newspaper, in which there had appeared several insulting articles upon a Mr. Stuart of Dunearn, a peaceable, well-esteemed man, who, however, was a Whig. Stuart, after having in vain tried to find out who was the author, had the MS. of one of the articles, severely handling his private character, brought to him by a needy partner in the concern (who, it is said, demanded £300 for the favour). The MS. was in Boswell's handwriting. Stuart challenged him, and though till the last moment Stuart urged him to apologise, the duel was fought (Boswell's second, the Hon. J. Douglas ; Stuart's, the Earl of Rosslyn). Boswell was wounded, and was carried to Lord Balmuto's house, Fifeshire, in whose grounds the duel took place ; and there died. We have heard from a gentleman, who was living in those circles at the time, that Boswell's conduct in the affair was altogether unjustifiable.

LIII.

THE LEA-RIG.

R. Fergusson.—Born 1750 ; Died 1774.

Will ye gang o'er the lea-rig
  My ain kind dearie, O ;
And cuddle there fu' kindly,
  Wi' me, my kind dearie, O !
At thorny dike and birken tree,
  We'll daff and ne'er be weary O ;
They'll scug ilk e'e frae you and me,
  My ain kind dearie, O.

Nae herds wi' kent or colly there,
  Shall ever come to fear ye, O ;
But lav'rocks whistling in the air
  Shall woo, like me, their dearie O.
While ithers herd their lambs and yowes,
  And toil for warld's gear, my jo,
Upon the lea my pleasure grows
  Wi' thee, my kind dearie, O.

Poor Fergusson's career was very short ; he died in a madhouse at four-and-twenty. Burns, it is well known,

as soon as he had extricated himself from his pressing
money difficulties, placed a simple stone on the grave of
this youth, whom he called his "elder Brother in misfortune."

LIV.

THE LEA-RIG.

R. Burns.

When o'er the hill the eastern star,
   Tells bughtin-time is near, my jo;
And owsen frae the furrowed field,
   Return sae dowf and weary, O;
Doun by the burn where scented birks
   Wi' dew are hanging clear, my jo;
I'll meet thee on the lea-rig,
   My ain kind dearie O !

In mirkest glen, at midnight hour,
   I'd rove, and ne'er be eerie, O;
If thro' that glen I gaed to thee,
   My ain kind dearie, O !
Altho' the night were ne'er sae wild,
   And I were ne'er sae wearie, O,
I'd meet thee on the lea-rig,
   My ain kind dearie, O !

The hunter lo'es the morning sun,
   To rouse the mountain deer, my jo;
At noon the fisher seeks the glen,
   Along the burn to steer, my jo;

Gie me the hour o' gloamin' gray,
   It maks my heart sae cheery, O,
To meet thee on the lea-rig,
   My ain kind dearie, O !

LV.

DOUN THE BURN, DAVIE.

R. Crawford.

When trees did bud, and fields were green,
   And broom bloom'd fair to see ;
When Mary was complete fifteen,
   And love laugh'd in her e'e ;
Blythe Davie's blinks her heart did move
   To speak her mind thus free,
Gang doun the burn, Davie, love,
   And I will follow thee.

Now Davie did each lad surpass
   That dwelt on this burnside ;
And Mary was the bonniest lass,
   Just meet to be a bride :
Her cheeks were rosie, red and white ;
   Her een were bonnie blue ;
Her looks were like Aurora bright,
   Her lips like dropping dew.

What pass'd, I guess, was harmless play,
   And naething sure unmeet ;
For ganging hame I heard them say,
   They liked a walk sae sweet ;

And that they often should return
    Sic' pleasure to renew.
Quoth Mary, Love, I like the burn,
    And aye shall follow you.

We have omitted one stanza of this song.

LVI.

O MALLY'S MEEK.

R. Burns.

As I was walking up the street,
    A barefit maid I chanc'd to meet;
But O the road was very hard
    For that fair maiden's tender feet.

        O Mally's meek, Mally's sweet,
            Mally's modest and discreet,
        Mally's rare, Mally's fair,
            Mally's every way complete.

It were mair meet, that those fine feet
    Were weel lac'd up in silken shoon,
And 'twere more fit that she should sit
    Within yon chariot gilt aboon.

Her yellow hair, beyond compare,
    Comes trinkling down her swan-white neck;
And her two eyes, like stars in skies,
    Would keep a sinking ship frae wreck.

LVII.

DAINTY DAVIE.

R. Burns.

Now rosy May comes in wi' flowers,
To deck her gay, green-spreading bowers,
And now come in my happy hours,
   To wander wi' my Davie.

     Meet me on the warlock knowe,
      Dainty Davie, dainty Davie;
     There I'll spend the day wi' you,
      My ain dear dainty Davie.

The crystal waters round us fa',
The merry birds are lovers a',
The scented breezes round us blaw,
   A-wandering wi' my Davie.

When purple morning starts the hare,
To steal upon her early fare,
Then through the dews I will repair,
   To meet my faithfu' Davie.

When day, expiring in the west,
The curtain draws o' Nature's rest,
I'll flee to his arms I lo'e best,
   And that's my dainty Davie.

LVIII.

I LOVE MY JEAN.

R. Burns.

Of a' the airts the wind can blaw,
   I dearly like the west;
For there the bonnie lassie lives,
   The lassie I lo'e best:
There wild-woods grow, and rivers row,
   And monie a hill between,
But day and night, my fancy's flight
   Is ever wi' my Jean.

I see her in the dewy flowers,
   I see her sweet and fair;
I hear her in the tunefu' birds,
   I hear her charm the air.
There's not a bonnie flow'r that springs,
   By fountain, shaw, or green;
There's not a bonnie bird that sings,
   But minds me o' my Jean.

LIX.

THEIR GROVES O' SWEET MYRTLE.

R. Burns.

Their groves o' sweet myrtle let foreign lands
    reckon,
   Where bright-beaming summers exalt the per-
   fume,

Far dearer to me yon lone glen o' green breckan,
  Wi' the burn stealing under the lang yellow
      broom ;
Far dearer to me are yon humble broom bowers,
  Where the blue-bell and gowan lurk lowly un-
      seen ;
For there, lightly tripping amang the wild flowers,
  A-listening the linnet, aft wanders my Jean.

Though rich is the breeze in their gay sunny
      valleys,
  And cauld, Caledonia's blast on the wave ;
Their sweet-scented woodlands that skirt the
      proud palace,
  What are they?   The haunt of the tyrant and
      slave !
The slave's spicy forests, and gold-bubbling foun-
      tains,
  The brave Caledonian views with disdain ;
He wanders as free as the winds of his moun-
      tains,
  Save love's willing fetters, the chains of his
      Jean !

LX.

SAE MERRY AS WE TWA HA'E BEEN.

A lass that was laden wi care
  Sat heavily under yon thorn ;

I listen'd a while for to hear,
   When thus she began for to mourn—
Whene'er my dear shepherd was there,
   The birds did melodiously sing,
And cold nipping winter did wear,
   A face that resembled the spring.

     Sae merry as we twa ha'e been,
       Sae merry as we twa ha'e been ;
     My heart is like for to break,
       When I think on the days we ha'e seen.

Our flocks feeding close by our side,
   He gently pressing my hand,
I viewed the wide world in its pride,
   And laugh'd at the pomp of command !
My dear, he would oft to me say,
   What makes you hard-hearted to me ?
Oh, why do you thus turn away,
   From him who is dying for thee ?

But now he is far from my sight,
   Perhaps a deceiver may prove,
Which makes me lament day and night,
   That ever I granted my love.
At eve, when the rest of the folk,
   Are merrily seated to spin,
I set myself under an oak,
   And heavily sigh for him.

This song "is beautiful; the chorus in particular is truly pathetic. I never could learn anything of its author."—*Burns.*

LXI.

JESSY.

R. Burns.

Here's a health to ane I lo'e dear,
Here's a health to ane I lo'e dear;
Thou art sweet as the smile when fond lovers
      meet,
And soft as their parting tear—Jessy!

Altho' thou maun never be mine,
   Altho' even hope is denied;
'Tis sweeter for thee despairing,
   Than ought in the world beside—Jessy!

I mourn through the gay, gaudy day,
   As, hopeless, I muse on thy charms;
But welcome the dream o' sweet slumber,
   For then I am lock'd in thy arms—Jessy!

I guess by the dear angel smile,
   I guess by the love-rolling e'e;
But why urge the tender confession,
   'Gainst fortune's fell cruel decree?—Jessy!

The Jessy of this, and several other songs, was Jessy
Lewars, sister of a fellow-exciseman of Burns' in Dumfries. She was distinguished from many of his contem-
porary admirers by the affectionate sympathy which she
always had for him and for his wife; and which, during
his last illness, took the form of a daughter's watchful
care. This is the last song Burns ever wrote.

LXII.

FOR LACK OF GOLD.

Adam Austin, M.D.—Born 1726? ; Died 1774.

For lack of gold she's left me, O,
And of all that's dear bereft me, O ;
She me forsook for Athole's duke,
    And to endless woe she has left me, O.
A star and garter have more art
Than youth, a true and faithful heart ;
For empty titles we must part,
    And for glittering show she's left me, O.

No cruel fair shall ever move
My injur'd heart again to love ;
Through distant climates I must rove ;
    Since Jeany she has left me, O.
Ye powers above, I to your care
Give up my faithless, lovely fair ;
Your choicest blessings be her share,
    Though she's for ever left me, O.

The cruel fair alluded to became the wife of James, Duke of Athole, and afterwards, having survived him, wife of Lord Adam Gordon. Dr. Austin did not " rove to distant climates," but continued to practise medicine in Edinburgh, where, some four or five years afterwards, he was married.

LXIII.

MY SHEEP I'VE FORSAKEN.

Sir Gilbert Elliot, Bart.—Born 1722 ; Died 1777.

My sheep I've forsaken, and left my sheep-hook,
And all the gay haunts of my youth I forsook ;

No more for Amynta fresh garlands I wove;
For ambition, I said, would soon cure me of love.

Oh, what had my youth with ambition to do?
Why left I Amynta? Why broke I my vow?
Oh, give me my sheep, and my sheep-hook
    restore,
And I'll wander from love and Amynta no more.

Through regions remote in vain do I rove,
And bid the wide ocean secure me from love!
Oh, fool! to imagine that aught could subdue
A love so well-founded, a passion so true!

Alas! 'tis too late at thy fate to repine;
Poor shepherd, Amynta can never be thine:
Thy tears are all fruitless, thy wishes are vain,
The moments neglected return not again.

LXIV.

STREPHON AND LYDIA.

William Wallace.—Born 1712?; Died 1763.

All lonely, on the sultry beach,
    Expiring Strephon lay;
No hand the cordial draught to reach,
    Nor cheer the gloomy way.
Ill-fated youth! no parent nigh
    To catch thy fleeting breath,
No bride to fix thy swimming eye,
    Or smooth the face of death.

Far distant from the mournful scene,
　Thy parents sit at ease;
Thy Lydia rifles all the plain,
　And all the spring, to please.
Ill-fated youth! by fault of friend,
　Not force of foe depress'd,
Thou fall'st, alas! thyself, thy kind,
　Thy country, unredress'd.

LXV.

CROMLET'S LILT.

Since all thy vows, false maid,
　Are blown to air,
And my poor heart betray'd
　To sad despair;
Into some wilderness
My grief I will express,
And thy hard-heartedness,
　Oh, cruel fair!

Have I not graven our loves
　On every tree
In yonder spreading groves,
　Though false thou be?
Was not a solemn oath
Plighted betwixt us both,
Thou thy faith, I my troth,
　Constant to be?

Some gloomy place I'll find,
  Some doleful shade,
Where neither sun nor wind
  E'er entrance had.
Into that hollow cave
There will I sigh and rave,
Because thou dost behave
  So faithlessly.

Wild fruit shall be my meat,
  I'll drink the spring ;
Cold earth shall be my seat ;
  For covering,
I'll have the starry sky
My head to canopy,
Until my soul on high
  Shall spread its wing.

I'll have no funeral fire,
  No tears for me ;
No grave do I require,
  Nor obsequies :
The courteous red-breast, he
With leaves will cover me,
And sing my elegy
  With doleful voice.

And when a ghost I am,
  I'll visit thee,
Oh, thou deceitful dame,
  Whose cruelty
Has kill'd the kindest heart
That e'er felt Cupid's dart,

And never can desert
From loving thee !

An interesting account of this song or dirge will be
found in *Burns' Reliques*, p. 226, *et seq.*

LXVI.

HAD I A CAVE.

R. Burns.

Had I a cave on some wild distant shore,
Where the winds howl to the waves' dashing roar :
    There would I weep my woes,
    There seek my lost repose,
    Till grief my eyes should close,
      Ne'er to wake more.

Falsest of womankind, canst thou declare,
All thy fond-plighted vows fleeting as air !
    To thy new lover hie,
    Laugh o'er thy perjury,
    Then in thy bosom try
      What peace is there !

LXVII.

MY MOTHER BIDS ME.

Anne Home, afterwards Mrs. Hunter.
Born 1742 ; Died 1821.

My mother bids me bind my hair
With bands of rosy hue,

Tie up my sleeves with ribbons rare,
    And lace my boddice blue.

For why, she cries, sit still and weep,
    While others dance and play?
Alas! I scarce can go or creep,
    While **Lubin** is away.

'Tis sad to think the days are gone,
    When those we love were near;
I sit upon this mossy stone,
    And sigh when none can hear.

And while I spin my flaxen thread,
    And sing my simple lay,
The village seems asleep, or dead,
    Now **Lubin** is away.

The authoress of this, and several other songs, was the wife of John Hunter of Glasgow, the celebrated anatomist and physiologist.

LXVIII.

TAM GLEN.

R. Burns.

My heart is a-breaking, dear Tittie!
    Some counsel unto me come len';
To anger them a' is a pity,
    But what will I do wi' Tam Glen?

I'm thinking wi' sic a braw fallow,
　In poortith I might mak' a fen :
What care I in riches to wallow,
　If I maunna marry Tam Glen?

There's Lowrie, the laird o' Drumeller,
　'Good day to you, brute!' he comes ben :
He brags and he blaws o' his siller,
　But when will he dance like Tam Glen?

My minnie does constantly deave me,
　And bids me beware o' young men ;
They flatter, she says, to deceive me,
　But wha can think sae o' Tam Glen?

My daddie says, gin I'll forsake him,
　He'll gie me gude hunder marks ten ;
But, if it's ordain'd I maun take him,
　O, wha will I get but Tam Glen?

Yestreen at the valentine's dealin',
　My heart to my mou' gied a sten ;
For thrice I drew ane without failin',
　And thrice it was written, Tam Glen.

The last Hallowe'en I was waukin'
　My drookit sark-sleeve, as ye ken ;
His likeness cam' up the house staukin',
　And the very gray breeks o' Tam Glen !

Come, counsel, dear Tittie, don't tarry ;
　I'll gie you my bonnie black hen,
Gif ye will advise me to marry
　The lad I lo'e dearly, Tam Glen.

LXIX.

BEWARE O' BONNIE ANN.

R. Burns.

Ye gallants bright, I rede ye right,
    Beware o' bonnie Ann,
Her comely face sae fu' o' grace,
    Your heart she will trepan.
Her een sae bright, like stars by night,
    Her skin is like the swan ;
Sae jimply laced her genty waist,
    That sweetly ye might span.

Youth, grace, and love, attendant move,
    And pleasure leads the van ;
In a' their charms, and conquering arms,
    They wait on bonnie Ann.
The captive bands may chain the hands,
    But love enslaves the man ;
Ye gallants braw, I rede ye a',
    · Beware o' bonnie Ann !

LXX.

I GAED A WAEFU' GATE.

R. Burns.

I gaed a waefu' gate yestreen,
    A gate, I fear, I'll dearly rue ;
I gat my death frae twa sweet een,
    Twa lovely een o' bonnie blue.

'Twas not her golden ringlets bright,
   Her lips, like roses wet wi' dew,
Her heaving bosom, lily-white,
   It was her een sae bonnie blue.

She talk'd, she smil'd, my heart she wil'd,
   She charm'd my soul, I wist na how,
And aye the stound, the deadly wound,
   Cam' frae her een sae bonnie blue,
But, spare to speak, and spare to speed,
   She'll aiblins listen to my vow ;
Should she refuse, I'll lay me dead
   To her twa een sae bonnie blue.

LXXI.

BONNIE LESLEY.

R. Burns.

O, saw ye bonnie Lesley,
   As she gaed o'er the border?
She's gane, like Alexander,
   To spread her conquests farther.

To see her is to love her,
   And love but her for ever ;
For nature made her what she is,
   And never made anither !

Thou art a queen, fair Lesley,
   Thy subjects we before thee :
Thou art divine, fair Lesley,
   The hearts o' men adore thee.

The deil he coudna scaith thee,
  Or aught that wad belang thee ;
He'd look into thy bonnie face,
  And say, ' I canna wrang thee !'

The powers aboon will tent thee ;
  Misfortune shanna steer thee ;
Thou'rt like themselves sae lovely,
  That ill they'll ne'er let near thee.

Return again, fair Lesley,
  Return to Caledonie !
That we may brag we ha'e a lass
  There's nane again sae bonnie.

LXXII.

LOGIE O' BUCHAN.

Attributed to George Halket.—Died 1756.

O Logie o' Buchan, O Logie the laird,
They ha'e ta'en awa' Jamie, that delved in the
      yard,
Wha play'd on the pipe, and the viol sae sma',
They ha'e ta'en awa Jamie, the flow'r o' them a'.

He said, Think na lang lassie, tho' I gang awa' ;
He said, Think na lang lassie, tho' I gang awa' ;
For simmer is coming, cauld winter's awa',
And I'll come and see thee in spite o' them a'.

Tho' Sandy has ousen, has gear, and has kye ;
A house, and a hadden, and siller forbye :
Yet I'd tak' my ain lad, wi' his staff in his hand,
Before I'd ha'e him, wi' the houses and land.

My daddie looks sulky, my minnie looks sour,
They frown upon Jamie because he is poor ;
Tho' I lo'e them as weel as a daughter should do,
They're nae hauf sae dear to me, Jamie, as you.

I sit on my creepie, I spin at my wheel,
And think on the laddie that lo'ed me sae weel :
He had but ae saxpence, he brak it in twa,
And gied me the hauf o't when he ga'ed awa',

Then haste ye back, Jamie, and bide na awa',
Then haste ye back, Jamie, and bide na awa',
The simmer is coming, cauld winter's awa',
And ye'll come and see me in spite o' them a'.

LXXIII.

LUCY'S FLITTING.

William Laidlaw.—Born 1780 ; Died 1845.

Twas when the wan leaf frae the birk tree was
        fa'in,
And Martinmas dowie had wound up the year,
That Lucy row'd up her wee kist wi' her a' in't,
And left her auld maister and neebours sae dear :

For Lucy had served in the glen a' the simmer;
She cam' there afore the flower bloomed on the
    pea;
An orphan she was, and they had been kind till
    her,
Sure that was the thing brocht the tear to her e'e.

She gaed by the stable where Jamie was stan'in';
Richt sair was his kind heart, the flittin' to see
Fare ye weel, Lucy! quo' Jamie, and ran in;
The gatherin' tears trickled fast frae his e'e.
As down the burn-side she gaed slow wi' the
    flittin',
Fare ye weel, Lucy! was ilka bird's sang;
She heard the craw sayin't, high on the tree
    sittin',
And robin was chirpin't the brown leaves amang.

Oh, what is't that pits my puir heart in a flutter?
And what gars the tears come sae fast to my e'e?
If I wasna ettled to be ony better,
Then what gars me wish ony better to be?
I'm just like a lammie that loses it's mither;
Nae mither or friend the puir lammie can see;
I fear I ha'e tint my puir heart a'thegither,
Nae wonder the tears fa' sae fast frae my e'e.

Wi' the rest o' my claes I ha'e row'd up the
    ribbon,
The bonnie blue ribbon that Jamie ga'e me;
Yestreen, when he ga'e me't, and saw I was
    sabbin',
I'll never forget the wae blink o' his e'e.

Though now he said naething but Fare ye weel,
    Lucy !
It made me I neither could speak, hear, nor see ;
He couldna say mair but just, Fare ye weel, Lucy !
Yet that I will mind till the day that I dee.

The lamb likes the gowan wi' dew when it's
    drookit ;
The hare likes the brake and the braird on the lea ;
But Lucy likes Jamie,—she turn'd and she lookit.
She thocht the dear place she wad never mair see.
Ah, weel may young Jamie gang dowie and
    cheerless !
And weel may he greet on the bank o' the burn !
For bonnie sweet Lucy, sae gentle and peerless,
Lies cauld in her grave, and will never return !

The author of this sweet little song was Scott's valued
friend and steward. On Scott's return to Abbotsford from
Naples, after having travelled from London in a state of
utter prostration and semi-unconsciousness, seeing Laidlaw
at his bedside, he said, his eyes brightening, " Is that
you, Willie ? I ken I'm hame noo."*

LXXIV.

WANDERING WILLIE.

R. Burns.

Here awa', there awa', wandering Willie,
    Here awa', there awa', haud awa' hame ;

---

* *The Songs of England and Scotland* (London, 1835),
Vol. II., p. 325.

Come to my bosom, my ain only dearie,
  Tell me thou bring'st me my Willie the same.

Winter winds blew loud and cauld at our parting;
  Fears for my Willie brought tears in my e'e;
Welcome now, simmer, and welcome, my Willie,
  The simmer to nature, my Willie to me.

Rest, ye wild storms, in the caves o' your slum-
       bers;
  How your dread howling a lover alarms!
Wauken, ye breezes! row gently, ye billows!
  And waft my dear laddie ance mair to my
       arms.

But, oh, if he's faithless, and minds na his Nannie,
  Flow still between us, thou wide, roaring main;
May I never see it, may I never trow it,
  But, dying, believe that my Willie's my ain!

LXXV.

AULD ROB MORRIS.

R. Burns.

There's auld Rob Morris, that wons in yon glen,
He's the king o' gude fellows, and wale of auld
      men;
He has gowd in his coffers, and owsen and kine,
And ae bonnie lassie, his darling and mine.

She's fresh as the morning, the fairest in May;
She's sweet as the ev'ning amang the new hay;
As blythe and as artless as the lambs on the lea,
And dear to my heart as the licht to my e'e.

But, oh, she's an heiress, auld Robin's a laird,
And my daddie has nocht but a cot-house and
    yard;
A wooer like me maunna hope to come speed;
The wounds I maun hide that will soon be my
    deid.

The day comes to me, but delight brings me nane;
The nicht comes to me, but my rest it is gane;
I wander my lane, like a nicht-troubled ghaist,
And I sigh as my heart it wad burst in my breast.

Oh, had she but been of a lower degree,
I then micht ha'e hop'd she wad smil'd upon me!
Oh, how past describing had then been my bliss,
As now my distraction no words can express!

There is an older *Rob Morris* (Burns has taken his
two first lines from it); which, however, would be less
appropriate here than the one given.

LXXVI.

MY BONNIE MARY.

R. Burns.

Go fetch to me a pint o' wine,
    An' fill it in a silver tassie;
That I may drink, before I go,
    A service to my bonnie lassie.
The boat rocks at the pier o' Leith,
    Fu' loud the wind blaws frae the ferry;
The ship rides by the Berwick Law;
    And I maun leave my bonnie Mary.

The trumpets sound, the banners fly ;
  The glittering spears are ranked ready :
The shouts o' war are heard afar ;
  The battle closes thick and bloody :
But it's not the roar o' sea or shore
  Would mak' me langer wish to tarry ;
Nor shouts of war, that's heard afar,
  It's leaving thee, my bonnie Mary.

LXXVII.

CRADLE SONG.

Richard Gall.—Born 1766 ; Died 1801.

Baloo, baloo, my wee wee thing,
  O saftly close thy blinking e'e !
Baloo, baloo, my wee wee thing,
  For thou art doubly dear to me.
Thy daddie now is far awa',
  A sailor laddie o'er the sea ;
But Hope aye hechts his safe return
  To you, my bonnie lamb, an' me.

Baloo, baloo, my wee wee thing,
  O saftly close thy blinking e'e !
Baloo, baloo, my wee wee thing,
  For thou art doubly dear to me.
Thy face is simple, sweet, an' mild,
  Like ony simmer e'ening fa',
Thy sparkling e'e is bonnie black,
  Thy neck is like the mountain snaw.

Baloo, baloo, my wee wee thing,
  O saftly close thy blinkin' e'e !
Baloo, baloo, my wee wee thing,
  For thou art doubly dear to me.
O but thy daddie's absence lang,
  Might break my dowie heart in twa,
Wert thou no left a dawtit pledge,
  To steal the eerie hours awa'.

LXXVIII.

WILT THOU BE MY DEARIE.

R. Burns.

Wilt thou be my dearie?
When sorrow wrings thy gentle heart,
Wilt thou let me cheer thee?
By the treasures of my soul,
That's the love I bear thee !
I swear and vow that only thou
Shall ever be my dearie.
Only thou, I swear and vow,
Shall ever be my dearie.

Lassie, say thou lo'es me,
Or if thou wilt not be my ain,
Say na thou'lt refuse me :
If it winna, canna be,
Thou for thine may choose me,
Let me, lassie, quickly die,
Trusting that thou lo'es me.
Lassie, let me quickly die,
Trusting that thou lo'es me.

LXXIX.

RED GLEAMS THE SUN.

R. Couper, M.D.—Born 1750; Died 1818.

Red gleams the sun on yon hill tap,
   The dew sits on the gowan;
Deep murmurs through her glens the Spey,
   Around Kinrara rowan.
Where art thou, fairest, kindest lass?
   Alas! wert thou but near me,
Thy gentle soul, thy melting eye,
   Would ever, ever cheer me.

The lav'rock sings amang the clouds,
   The lambs they sport so cheery,
And I sit weeping by the birk,
   O where art thou my deary?
Aft may I meet the morning dew,
   Lang greet till I be weary,
Thou canna, winna, gentle maid,
   Thou canna be my deary.

LXXX.

MY NANNIE, O.

R. Burns.

Behind yon hills where Lugar flows,
   'Mang moors and mosses many, O,

The wintry sun the day has clos'd,
   And I'll awa' to Nannie, O.
The westlin wind blaws loud and shrill
   The night's baith mirk and rainy, O,
But I'll get my plaid, and out I'll steal,
   And o'er the hills to Nannie, O.

My Nannie's charming, sweet, and young;
   Nae artfu' wiles to win ye, O ;
May ill befa' the flattering tongue
   That wad beguile my Nannie, O.
Her face is fair, her heart is true,
   And spotless as she's bonnie, O ;
The opening gowan wat wi' dew,
   Nae purer is than Nannie, O.

A country lad is my degree,
   And few there be that ken me, O ;
But what care I how few they be?
   I'm welcome aye to Nannie, O.
My riches a's my penny fee,
   And I maun guide it cannie, O ;
But warl's gear ne'er troubles me,
   My thoughts are a' my Nannie, O.

Our auld gudeman delights to view
   His sheep and kye thrive bonnie, O ;
But I'm as blythe that hauds his pleugh,
   And has nae care but Nannie, O.
Come weel, come woe, I carena by,
   I'll tak' what heaven will send me, O ;
Nae ither care in life have I,
   But live and love my Nannie, O.

LXXXI.

THE LASS O' ARRANTEENIE.

Robert Tannahill.—Born 1774; Died 1810.

Far lone amang the Highland hills,
  Midst nature's wildest grandeur,
By rocky dens and woody glens,
  With weary steps I wander.
The langsome way, the darksome day,
  The mountain, misty, rainy,
Are naught to me, when gaun to thee,
  Sweet lass o' Arranteenie.

Yon mossy rose-bud down the howe,
  Just opening fresh and bonny,
It blinks beneath the hazel bough,
  And's scarcely seen by ony.
Sae sweet amidst her native hills,
  Obscurely blooms my Jeanie,
Mair fair and gay than rosy May,
  The flower o' Arranteenie.

Now from the mountains lofty brow,
  I view the distant ocean,
There avarice guides the bounding prow,
  Ambition courts promotion.
Let fortune pour her golden store,
  Her laurell'd favours many,
Give me but this, my soul's first wish,
  The lass o' Arranteenie.

Arranteenie, or Ardentinny, is beautifully situated on
the banks of Loch Long.

LXXXII.

GLOOMY WINTER.

R. Tannahill.

Gloomy winter's now awa',
Saft the westlin' breezes blaw :
'Mang the birks o' Stanley-shaw
   The mavis sings fu' cheerie, O.
Sweet the craw-flower's early bell
Decks Gleniffer's dewy dell,
Blooming like thy bonnie sel',
   My young, my artless dearie, O.

Come, my lassie, let us stray
O'er Glenkilloch's sunny brae,
Blythly spend the gowden day
   'Midst joys that never wearie, O.
Towering o'er the Newton woods,
Laverocks fan the snaw-white clouds ;
Siller saughs, wi' downie buds,
   Adorn the banks sae brierie, O.

Round the sylvan fairy nooks,
Feath'ry breckens fringe the rocks,
'Neath the brae the burnie jouks,
   And ilka thing is cheerie, O.
Trees may bud, and birds may sing,
Flowers may bloom, and verdure spring,
Joy to me they canna bring,
   Unless wi' thee, my dearie, O.

LXXXIII.

THE ROWAN TREE.

*Carolina Oliphant, afterwards Lady Nairne.
Born 1766; Died 1845.*

Oh, Rowan tree! Oh, Rowan tree! thou'lt aye
 be dear to me,
Intwined thou art wi' mony ties o' hame and
 infancy.
Thy leaves were aye the first o' spring, thy flowr's
 the simmer's pride;
There was na sic a bonnie tree in a' the countrie
 side.

How fair wert thou in simmer time, wi' a' thy
 clusters white,
How rich and gay thy autumn dress, wi' berries
 red and bright,
On thy fair stem were mony names, which now
 nae mair I see,
But they're engraven on my heart, forgot they
 ne'er can be!

We sat aneath thy spreading shade, the bairnies
 round thee ran;
They pu'd thy bonnie berries red, and necklaces
 they strang;
My mither, oh, I see her still! she smil'd our
 sports to see;
Wi' little Jeanie on her lap, an' Jamie at her
 knee!

Oh ! there arose my father's prayer, in holy
      evening's calm,
How sweet was then my mother's voice, in the
      Martyr's psalm ;
Now a' are gane ! we meet nae mair, aneath the
      Rowan tree,
But hallowed thoughts around thee twine o' hame
      and infancy.

LXXXIV.

CRAIGIE-LEA.

R. Tannahill.

Thou bonnie wood of Craigie-lea,
    Thou bonnie wood of Craigie-lea,
Near thee I pass'd life's early day,
    And won my Mary's heart in thee.

The broom, the brier, the birken bush,
    Bloom bonnie o'er thy flowery lea,
An' a' the sweets that ane can wish
    Frae nature's hand, are strew'd on thee.

Far ben thy dark-green planting's shade,
    The cushat croodles am'rously,
The mavis, down thy buchted glade,
    Gars echo ring frae every tree.

Awa', ye thoughtless, murd'ring gang,
    Wha tear the nestlings ere they flee !

They'll sing ye yet a canty sang,
  Then, O in pity let them be !

When winter blaws in sleety showers,
  Frae aff the Norlan' hills sae hie,
He lightly skiffs thy bonnie bowers,
  As laith to harm a flower in thee.

Though fate should drag me south the line,
  Or o'er the wide Atlantic sea ;
The happy hours I'll ever min'
  That I in youth hae spent in thee.

LXXXV.

O JEANIE.

James Hogg.—Born 1770 ; Died 1835.

O my lassie ! our joy to complete again,
  Meet me again in the gloamin', my dearie ;
Low down i' the dell let us meet again,
  O Jeanie ! there's naething to fear ye.
Come when the wee bat flits silent an eerie ;
Come when the pale face o' nature looks weary,
    Love be thy sure defence,
    Beauty and innocence—
O Jeanie ! there's naething to fear ye.

Sweetly blows the haw and the rowan-tree,
  Wild roses speck our thicket sae breerie ;
Still, still will our bed in the greenwood be—
  O Jeanie ! there's naething to fear ye :

Note when the blackbird o' singing grows weary,
List when the beetle-bee's bugle comes near ye :
    Then come with fairy haste,
    Light foot and beating breast—
O Jeanie ! there's naething to fear ye.

LXXXVI.

PHILLIS THE FAIR.

R. Burns.

    While larks with little wing
      Fann'd the pure air,
    Tasting the breathing spring,
      Forth I did fare ;
    Gay the sun's golden eye,
    Peep'd o'er the mountains high ;
    Such thy morn ! did I cry,
      Phillis the fair.

    In each bird's careless song,
      Glad did I share ;
    While yon wild flowers among,
      Chance led me there :
    Sweet to the opening day,
    Rosebuds bent the dewy spray ;
    Such thy bloom ! did I say,
      Phillis the fair.

    Down in a shady walk,
      Doves cooing were :
    I mark'd the cruel hawk
      Caught in a snare :

So kind may fortune be,
Such make his destiny !
He who would injure thee,
Phillis the fair.

LXXXVII.

ODE TO THE CUCKOO.

John Logan.

Hail, beauteous stranger of the grove !
Thou messenger of spring !
Now heaven repairs thy rural seat,
And woods thy welcome sing.

What time the daisy decks the green,
Thy certain voice we hear :
Hast thou a star to guide thy path,
Or mark the rolling year ?

Delightful visitant ! with thee
I hail the time of flowers,
And hear the sound of music sweet
From birds among the bowers.

The school-boy, wandering through the wood,
To pull the primrose gay,
Starts the new voice of spring to hear,
And imitates thy lay.

What time the pea puts on the bloom,
Thou fliest thy vocal vale,

An annual guest in other lands,
  Another spring to hail.

Sweet bird thy bower is ever green,
  Thy sky is ever clear;
Thou hast no sorrow in thy song,
  No winter in thy year !

Oh could I fly, I'd fly with thee !
  We'd make, with joyful wing,
Our annual visit o'er the globe,
  Companions of the spring.

LXXXVIII.

THE SKY-LARK.

James Hogg.

Bird of the wilderness,
  Blythesome and cumberless,
Sweet be thy matin o'er moorland and lea !
  Emblem of happiness,
  Blest is thy dwelling-place,
O, to abide in the desert with thee !

Wild is thy lay and loud,
  Far in the downy cloud ;
Love gives it energy, love gave it birth ;
  Where, on thy dewy wing,
  Where art thou journeying?
Thy lay is in heaven, thy love is on earth.

O'er fell and fountain sheen,
O'er moor and mountain green,
O'er the red streamer that heralds the day,
Over the cloudlet dim,
Over the rainbow's rim,
Musical cherub, soar, singing, away.

Then, when the gloaming comes,
Low in the heather blooms,
Sweet will thy welcome and bed of love be !
Emblem of happiness,
Blest is thy dwelling-place,
O, to abide in the desert with thee.

LXXXIX.

NANCY.

R. Burns.

Thine am I, my faithful fair,
Thine, my lovely Nancy ;
Ev'ry pulse along my veins,
Ev'ry roving fancy.

To thy bosom lay my heart,
There to throb and languish :
Though despair had wrung its core,
That would heal its anguish.

Take away these rosy lips,
Rich with balmy treasure ;

'Turn away thine eyes of love,
 Lest I die with pleasure.

What is life when wanting love?
 Night without a morning:
Love's the cloudless summer sun,
 Nature gay adorning.

XC.

FAIR MODEST FLOWER.

William Reid.—Born 1764; Died 1831.

Fair modest flower, of matchless worth!
 Thou sweet, enticing, bonnie gem,
Blest is the soil that gave thee birth,
 And blest thine honour'd parent stem.
But doubly blest shall be the youth,
 To whom thy heaving bosom warms;
Possess'd of beauty, love and truth,
 He'll clasp an angel in his arms.

Though storms of life were blowing snell,
 And on his brow sat brooding care,
Thy seraph smile would quick dispel
 The darkest gloom of black despair.
Sure heaven hath granted thee to us,
 And chose thee from the dwellers there,
And sent thee from celestial bliss,
 To show what all the virtues are.

XCI.

James Thomson.—Born 1700; Died 1748.

Come, gentle god of soft desire,
    Come and possess my happy breast,
Not fury-like in flames and fire,
    Or frantic folly's wildness drest;

But come in friendship's angel-guise;
    Yet dearer thou than friendship art,
More tender spirit in thy eyes,
    More sweet emotions at thy heart.

O come with goodness in thy train,
    With peace and pleasure void of storm,
And would'st thou me for ever gain,
    Put on Amanda's winning form.

XCII.

TALK NOT OF LOVE.

*Agnes Craig, afterwards Mrs. M'Lehose.
Born 1759; Died about 1841.*

Talk not of love, it gives me pain,
    For love has been my foe;
He bound me with an iron chain,
    And plunged me deep in woe.
But friendship's pure and lasting joys,
    My heart was formed to prove;
There, welcome, win and wear the prize,
    But never talk of love.

Your friendship much can make me blest,
    Oh, why that bliss destroy !
Why urge the only, one request
    You know I will deny !
Your thought, if love must harbour there,
    Conceal it in that thought ;
Nor cause me from my bosom tear
    The very friend I sought.

The authoress of this song,—the ' Clarinda,' whom
Burns has made famous,—is also the heroine of the one
which follows, as well as of several other songs. A touch-
ing account of her life will be found in the *Correspondence
between Burns and Clarinda* (Edin., 1843) ; a book well
worth reading, not only on this ground, but as illustrative
of an interesting section of Burns's life.

XCIII.

AE FOND KISS.

R. Burns.

Ae fond kiss, and then we sever ;
Ae farewell, alas, for ever !
Deep in heart-wrung tears I'll pledge thee,
Warring sighs and groans I'll wage thee.
Who shall say that fortune grieves him
While the star of hope she leaves him ?
Me, nae cheerfu' twinkle lights me ;
Dark despair around benights me.

I'll ne'er blame my partial fancy,
Naething could resist my Nancy ;

But to see her, was to love her;
Love but her, and love for ever.
Had we never loved sae kindly,
Had we never loved sae blindly,
Never met—or never parted,
We had ne'er been broken-hearted.

Fare thee weel, thou first and fairest!
Fare thee weel, thou best and dearest!
Thine be ilka joy and treasure,
Peace, enjoyment, love, and pleasure!
Ae fond kiss, and then we sever;
Ae farewell, alas, for ever!
Deep in heart-wrung tears I'll pledge thee,
Warring sighs and groans I'll wage thee!

"The following exquisitely affecting stanza contains the essence of a thousand love tales :—

> 'Had we never loved sae kindly,
> Had we never loved sae blindly,
> Never met—or never parted,
> We had ne'er been broken-hearted.'"—SCOTT.

Byron adopts this same stanza as motto to *The Bride of Abydos.*

XCIV.

I'LL NEVER LOVE THEE MORE.

*Attributed to James, Marquis of Montrose.
Born 1612; Executed 1650.*

My dear and only love, I pray
This little world of thee
Be govern'd by no other sway,
But purest monarchy;

For if confusion have a part,
  Which virtuous souls abhor,
I'll call a synod in my heart,
  And never love thee more.

As Alexander I will reign,
  And I will reign alone,
My thoughts shall evermore disdain
  A rival on my throne.
He either fears his fate too much,
  Or his deserts are small,
Who puts it not unto the touch,
  To win or lose it all.

But I must rule and govern still,
  And always give the law;
And have each subject at my will,
  And all to stand in awe:
But 'gainst my batteries if I find
  Thou storm, or vex me sore,
Or if thou set me as a blind,
  I'll never love thee more.

Or in the empire of thy heart,
  Where I should solely be,
Another do pretend a part,
  And dare to vie with me;
Or if committees thou erect,
  Or go on such a score,
I'll sing and laugh at thy neglect,
  And never love thee more.

But if thou wilt be constant then,
  And faithful to thy word,

I'll make thee famous by my pen
And glorious by my sword.
I'll serve thee in such noble ways,
As ne'er were known before :
I'll crown and deck thy head with bays
And love thee more and more.

xcv.

INCONSTANCY REPROVED.

Attributed to Sir Robert Aytoun.—Born 1570 ; Died 1638.

I do confess thou'rt smooth and fair,
And I might have gone near to love thee,
Had I not found the slightest pray'r
That lips could speak, had power to move thee,
But I can let thee now alone,
As worthy to be lov'd by none.

I do confess thou'rt sweet, yet find
Thee such an unthrift of thy sweets,
Thy favours are but like the wind,
That kisseth everything it meets ;
And since thou can'st love more than one,
Thou'rt worthy to be lov'd by none.

The morning rose that untouch'd stands,
Arm'd with her briars, how sweetly smells,
But, pluck'd and strain'd through ruder hands,
Her charm no longer with her dwells,
But scent and beauty both are gone,
And leaves fall from her one by one.

Such fate e're long will thee betide,
   When thou hast handled been awhile;
Like fair flowers to be thrown aside,
   And thou shalt sigh when I shall smile
     To see thy love to every one,
     Hath brought thee to be lov'd by none.

XCVI.

THERE WAS A LASS.

R. Burns.

There was a lass, and she was fair,
   At kirk and market to be seen,
When a' the fairest maids were met,
   The fairest maid was bonnie Jean.

And aye she wrought her mammie's wark,
   And aye she sang sae merrilie:
The blithest bird upon the bush
   Had ne'er a lighter heart than she.

But hawks will rob the tender joys
   That bless the little lintwhite's nest;
And frost will blight the fairest flowers,
   And love will break the soundest rest.

Young Robie was the brawest lad,
   The flower and pride of a' the glen:
And he had owsen, sheep, and kye,
   And wanton naigies nine or ten.

He gaed wi' Jeanie to the tryste,
  He danc'd wi' Jeanie on the down ;
And lang ere witless Jeanie wist,
  Her heart was tint, her peace was stown.

As in the bosom o' the stream,
  The moonbeam dwells at dewy e'en ;
So trembling, pure, was tender love,
  Within the breast o' bonnie Jean.

And now she works her mammie's wark,
  And aye she sighs wi' care and pain ;
Yet wist'na what her ail might be,
  Or what wad mak' her weel again.

But didna Jeanie's heart loup light,
  And didna joy blink in her e'e,
As Robie tauld a tale o' love,
  Ae e'enin' on the lily lea?

The sun was sinking in the west,
  The birds sang sweet in ilka grove ;
His cheek to her's he fondly prest,
  And whisper'd thus his tale o' love :

O Jeanie fair, I lo'e thee dear ;
  O canst thou think to fancy me ;
Or wilt thou leave thy mammie's cot,
  And learn to tent the farms wi' me ?

At barn or byre thou shalt na drudge,
  Or naething else to trouble thee ;
But stray amang the heather-bells,
  And tent the waving corn wi' me.

Now what could artless Jeanie do?
   She had nae will to say him na :
At length she blush'd a sweet consent,
   And love was aye between them twa.

XCVII.

O TELL ME HOW TO WOO THEE.

Robert Graham of Gartmore.—Born 1750 ; Died 1797.

If doughty deeds my lady please,
   Right soon I'll mount my steed ;
And strong his arm, and fast his seat,
   That bears from me the meed.
I'll wear thy colours in my cap,
   Thy picture in my heart ;
And he that bends not to thine eye,
   Shall rue it to his smart !

     Then tell me how to woo thee, love,
       O tell me how to woo thee !
     For thy dear sake, nae care I'll take,
       Though ne'er another trow me.

If gay attire delight thine eye,
   I'll dight me in array ;
I'll tend thy chamber door all night,
   And squire thee all the day.
If sweetest sounds can win thine ear,
   These sounds I'll try to catch ;
Thy voice I'll steal to woo thysell,
   That voice that nane can match.

But if fond love thy heart can gain,
  I never broke a vow ;
Nae maiden lays her skaith to me ;
  I never loved but you.
For you alone I ride the ring,
  For you I wear the blue ;
For you alone I strive to sing—
  O tell me how to woo !

XCVIII.

PINKIE HOUSE.

Joseph Mitchell.—Born 1684; Died 1734.

By Pinkie House oft let me walk,
  While, circled in my arms,
I hear my Nelly sweetly talk,
  And gaze on all her charms.
O let me ever fond behold
  Those graces void of art,
Those cheerful smiles that sweetly hold,
  In willing chains, my heart !

O come, my love ! and bring anew
  That gentle turn of mind ;
That gracefulness of air, in you
  By nature's hand design'd.
That beauty like the blushing rose,
  First lighted up this flame,
Which, like the sun, for ever glows
  Within my breast the same.

Ye light coquettes ! ye airy things !
   How vain is all your art,
How seldom it a lover brings,
   How rarely keeps a heart !
O gather from my Nelly's charms
   That sweet, that graceful ease,
That blushing modesty that warms,
   That native art to please !

Come then, my love ! O, come along !
   And feed me with thy charms ;
Come, fair inspirer of my song !
   Oh, fill my longing arms !
A flame like mine can never die,
   While charms so bright as thine,
So heavenly fair, both please the eye,
   And fill the soul divine !

XCIX.

MY AIN FIRESIDE.

Elizabeth Hamilton.—Died 1816, aged 67.

I ha'e seen great anes, and sat in great ha's,
Mang lords and fine ladies a' cover'd wi' braws ;
At feasts made for princes, wi' princes I've been,
Whare the grand shine o' splendour has dazzled
         my e'en ;

But a sight sae delightfu', I trow, I ne'er spied,
As the bonnie blythe blink o' my ain fireside.
My ain fireside, my ain fireside,
O cheery's the blink o' mine ain fireside.
   My ain fireside, my ain fireside,
    O there's nought to compare wi' ane's ain
     fireside.

Ance mair, gude be thanket, round my ain
    heartsome ingle,
Wi' the friends o' my youth I can cordially mingle;
Nae forms to compel me to seem wae or glad,
I may laugh when I'm merry, and sigh when
    I'm sad.
Nae falsehood to dread, and nae malice to fear,
But truth to delight me, and friendship to cheer;
Of a' roads to happiness ever were tried,
There's nane half so sure as ane's ain fireside.
   My ain fireside, my ain fireside,
    O there's nought to compare wi' ane's ain
     fireside.

When I draw in my stool on my cosey hearth-
    stane,
My heart loups sae light I scarce ken't for my
    ain;
Care's down on the wind, it is clean out o' sight,
Past troubles they seem but as dreams of the
    night.
I hear but kend voices, kend faces I see,
And mark saft affection glent fond frae ilk e'e;
Nae fleechings o' flattery, nae boastings of pride,

'Tis heart speaks to heart at ane's ain fireside.
  My ain fireside, my ain fireside,
    O there's nought to compare wi' ane's ain
      fireside.

This song is by the authoress of *The Cottagers of Glen-
burnie*, a genial and well-known Scotch story.

C.

BIDE YE YET.

Gin I had a wee house and a canty wee fire,
A bonnie wee wife to praise and admire;
A bonnie wee yardie aside a wee burn,
Farewell to the bodies that yammer and mourn.

      And bide ye yet, and bide ye yet,
        Ye little ken what may betide ye yet;
      Some bonnie wee bodie may fa' to my lot,
        And I'll aye be canty wi' thinking o't.

When I gang a-field, and come hame at e'en,
I'll get my wee wifie fu' neat and fu' clean;
And a bonnie wee bairnie upon her knee,
That will cry papa or daddy to me.

And if there should happen ever to be
A difference a'tween my wee wifie and me;
In hearty good humour, although she be teaz'd,
I'll kiss her and clap her until she be pleas'd.

From David Herd's Collection (Glasgow, 1776).

CI.

WHEN THE KYE COME HAME.

James Hogg.

Come all ye jolly shepherds
  That whistle through the glen,
I'll tell ye of a secret
  That courtiers dinna ken.
What is the greatest bliss
  That the tongue o' man can name?
'Tis to woo a bonnie lassie
  When the kye come hame.

    When the kye come hame,
      When the kye come hame,
    'Tween the gloamin and the mirk,
      When the kye come hame.

'Tis not beneath the burgonet,
  Nor yet beneath the crown,
'Tis not on couch of velvet,
  Nor yet on bed of down:
'Tis beneath the spreading birk,
  In the dell without a name,
Wi' a bonnie, bonnie lassie,
  When the kye come hame.

Then the eye shines sae bright,
  The haill soul to beguile,
There's love in every whisper,
  And joy in every smile;

O, who would choose a crown,
   Wi' its perils and its fame,
And miss a bonnie lassie
   When the kye come hame?

See yonder pawky shepherd
   That lingers on the hill—
His yowes are in the fauld,
   And his lambs are lying still ;
Yet he downa gang to rest,
   For his heart is in a flame
To meet his bonnie lassie
   When the kye come hame.

Awa' wi' fame and fortune ;
   What comfort can they gie?
And a' the arts that prey
   On man's life and libertie !
Gi'e me the highest joy
   That the heart o' man can frame ;
My bonnie, bonnie lassie,
   When the kye come hame.

CII.

WHEN I UPON THY BOSOM LEAN.

John Lapraik.—Born 1717 ; Died 1807.

When I upon thy bosom lean,
   And fondly clasp thee a' my ain,

I glory in the sacred ties
   That made us ane, wha ance were twain !
A mutual flame inspires us baith,
   The tender look, the melting kiss :
Even years shall ne'er destroy our love,
   But only gi'e us change o' bliss.

Ha'e I a wish ? it's a' for thee ;
   I ken thy wish is me to please ;
Our moments pass sae smooth away,
   That numbers on us look and gaze ;
Weel pleas'd they see our happy days,
   Nor envy's sel' finds aught to blame ;
And aye, when weary cares arise,
   Thy bosom still shall be my hame.

I'll lay me there and take my rest,
   And, if that aught disturb my dear,
I'll bid her laugh her cares away,
   And beg her not to shed a tear.
Ha'e I a joy; it's a' her ain;
   United still her heart and mine ;
They're like the woodbine round the tree,
   That's twin'd till death shall them disjoin.

Burns alludes to this song in a rhyming letter addressed
to its author :

> "There was ae sang amang the rest,
>   Aboon them a' it pleased me best,
>   That some kind husband had addrest
>   To some sweet wife :
> It thrill'd the heart-strings thro' the breast,
>   A' to the life."

CIII.

THE DAY RETURNS.

R. Burns.

The day returns, my bosom burns,
  The blissful day we twa did meet;
Though winter wild in tempest toil'd,
  Ne'er summer-sun was half sae sweet.
Than a' the pride that loads the tide,
  And crosses o'er the sultry line;
Than kingly robes, than crowns and globes,
  Heaven gave me more—it made thee mine!

While day and night can bring delight,
  Or nature aught of pleasure give,
While joys above my mind can move,
  For thee, and thee alone, I'll live!
When that grim foe of life below
  Comes in between to make us part;
The iron hand that breaks our band,
  It breaks my bliss—it breaks my heart.

CIV.

THERE'S NAE LUCK ABOUT THE HOUSE.

And are ye sure the news is true?
  And are ye sure he's weel?
Is this a time to talk of wark?
  Ye jauds, fling by your wheel.

Is this a time to talk o' wark,
  When Colin's at the door?
Gie me my cloak! I'll to the quay,
  And see him come ashore.

    For there's nae luck about the house,
      There's nae luck ava;
      There's little pleasure in the house,
      When our gudeman's awa.

Rise up and mak' a clean fireside;
  Put on the muckle pot;
Gi'e little Kate her cotton gown,
  And Jock his Sunday coat:
And mak' their shoon as black as slaes,
  Their hose as white as snaw;
It's a' to please my ain gudeman,
  For he's been lang awa'.

There's twa fat hens upon the bauk,
  Been fed this month and mair;
Mak' haste and thraw their necks about,
  That Colin weel may fare;
And mak' the table neat and clean,
  Gar ilka thing look braw;
It's a' for love of my gudeman,
  For he's been lang awa'.

O gi'e me down my bigonet,
  My bishop satin gown,
For I maun tell the bailie's wife
  That Colin's come to town.
My Sunday's shoon they maun gae on,
  My hose o' pearl blue;

'Tis a' to please my ain gudeman,
    For he's baith leal and true.

Sae true his words, sae smooth his speech,
    His breath's like caller air!
His very foot has music in't,
    As he comes up the stair.
And will I see his face again?
    And will I hear him speak?
I'm downright dizzy with the thought,—
    In troth, I'm like to greet.

The cauld blasts o' the winter wind,
    That thrilled through my heart,
They're a' blawn by; I ha'e him safe,
    Till death we'll never part:
But what puts parting in my head?
    It may be far awa';
The present moment is our ain,
    The neist we never saw.

Since Colin's well, I'm well content,
    I ha'e nae mair to crave;
Could I but live to mak' him blest,
    I'm blest aboon the lave:
And will I see his face again?
    And will I hear him speak?
I'm downright dizzy wi' the thought,—
    In troth, I'm like to greet.

"This is one of the most beautiful songs in the Scots
or any other language".—*Burns.*

It is uncertain who was the author, whether 'W. J.
Mickle,' to whom it is oftener ascribed, or 'Jean Adams,'
who is understood to have claimed it as hers.

CV.

THE BOATIE ROWS.

John Ewen.—Born 1741 ; Died 1821.

O weel may the boatie row,
  And better may she speed ;
And leesome may the boatie row.
  That wins the bairns's bread !
The boatie rows, the boatie rows,
  The boatie rows indeed,
And weel may the boatie row,
  That wins my bairns's bread.

I cust my line in Largo Bay,
  And fishes I caught nine ;
There's three to boil, and three to fry,
  And three to bait the line.
The boatie rows, the boatie rows,
  The boatie rows indeed ;
And happy be the lot of a'
  That wishes her to speed !

O weel may the boatie row,
  That fills a heavy creel,
And cleads us a' frae head to feet.
  And buys our parritch meal.
The boatie rows, the boatie rows,
  The boatie rows indeed ;
And happy be the lot of a'
  That wish the boatie speed.

When Jamie vow'd he would be mine,
  And wan frae me my heart,
O muckle lighter grew my creel!
  He swore we'd never part.
The boatie rows, the boatie rows,
  The boatie rows fu' weel;
And muckle lighter is the load,
  When love bears up the creel.

My kurtch I put upon my head,
  And dress'd mysel' fu' braw;
I trow my heart was dowf and wae,
  When Jamie gaed awa:
But weel may the boatie row,
  And lucky be her part;
And lightsome be the lassie's care
  That yields an honest heart!

When Sawnie, Jock, and Janetie,
  Are up and gotten lear,
They'll help to gar the boatie row,
  And lighten a' our care.
The boatie rows, the boatie rows,
  The boatie rows fu' weel;
And lightsome be her heart that bears
  The murlain and the creel!

And when wi' age we are worn down,
  And hirpling round the door,
They'll row to keep us dry and warm,
  As we did them before:
Then, weel may the boatie row,
  That wins the bairns's bread;

And happy be the lot of a'
That wish the boat to speed !

"The 'Boatie Rows' is a charming display of womanly
affection mingling with the concerns and occupations of
life."—*Burns.*

CVI.

CALLER HERRIN'.

Lady Nairne.

Wha'll buy my caller herrin'?
They're bonnie fish and dainty fairin';
Wha'll buy my caller herrin'?
New drawn frae the Forth.

When ye were sleepin' on your pillows,
Dream'd ye aught of our puir fellows,
Darkling as they fac'd the billows,
A' to fill our woven willows?

Wha'll buy my caller herrin'?
They're no brought here without brave darin',
Buy my caller herrin',
Haul'd through wind and rain.

Wha'll buy my caller herrin'?
Ye may ca' them vulgar fairin';
Wives and mithers, maist despairin',
Ca' them lives o' men.

I

When the creel o' herrin' passes,
Ladies clad in silks and laces,
Gather in their braw pelisses,
Cast their necks and screw their faces.

Caller herrin's no got lightlie,
Ye can trip the spring fu' tightlie,
Spite o' tauntin', flauntin', flinging,
Gow has sent you a' a-singing.

Neighbour wives, now tent my tellin',
When the bonnie fish ye're sellin',
At ae word be in your dealin',
'Truth will stand when a' thing's failin'.

CVII.

TAK' YOUR AULD CLOAK ABOUT YOU.

In winter, when the rain rain'd cauld,
   And frost and snaw on ilka hill,
And Boreas, wi' his blasts sae bauld,
   Was threat'nin' a' our kye to kill:
Then Bell, my wife, wha lo'es nae strife,
   She said to me richt hastilie,
Get up, gudeman, save Crummie's life,
   And tak' your auld cloak about ye

My Crummie is a usefu' cow,
   And she is come of a good kin',
Aft has she wet the bairns's mou',
   And I am laith that she should tyne;

Get up, gudeman, it is fu' time,
  The sun shines frae the lift sae hie :
Sloth never made a gracious end ;
  Gae tak' your auld cloak about ye.

My cloak was ance a gude grey cloak,
  When it was fitting for my wear ;
But now it's scantly worth a groat,
  For I have worn't this thretty year :
Let's spend the gear that we ha'e won,
  We little ken the day we'll die ;
Then I'll be proud, since I have sworn
  To ha'e a new cloak about me.

In days when our King Robert rang,
  His trews they cost but half a croun ;
He said they were a groat ower dear,
  And ca'ed the tailor thief and loon :
He was the king that wore a croun,
  And thou the man of laigh degree :
'Tis pride puts a' the country doun ;
  Sae tak' your auld cloak about ye.

Ilka land has its ain laigh,*
  Ilk kind o' corn has its ain hool ;
I think the warld is a' gane wrang,
  When ilka wife her man wad rule :
Do ye no see Rob, Jock, and Hab,
  As they are girded gallantlie,
While I sit hurklin' in the asse ;
  I'll ha'e a new cloak about me.

* 'Laigh'—the undrainable portion of a farm, as useless as the ' hool' of the corn is.—*Kitson.*

Gudeman, I wat its thretty year
  Sin' we did ane anither ken ;
And we ha'e had atween us twa
  Of lads and bonnie lassies ten :
Now they are women grown and men,
  I wish and pray weel may they be ;
If you would prove a gude husband,
  E'en tak' your auld cloak about ye.

Bell, my wife, she lo'es nae strife,
  But she would guide me, if she can ;
And to maintain an easy life,
  I aft maun yield, though I'm gudeman :
Nocht's to be won at woman's hand,
  Unless ye gie her a' the plea ;
Then I'll leave aff where I began
  And tak' my auld cloak about me.

Percy, in his *Reliques of Ancient English Poetry*, prints
an English version of this song ; though he supposes it to
be originally Scotch. It will be remembered that Iago
sings, with only a few changes (as Stephen for Robert),
the fourth stanza beginning—

    " In days when our King Robert rang."

CVIII.

BLINK OVER THE BURN SWEET BETTY.

In summer I mawed my meadow,
  In harvest I shure my corn,
In winter I married a widow,
  I wish I was free the morn !

Blink o'er the burn, sweet Betty,
Blink o'er the burn to me :
Oh, it is a thousand pities
But I was a widow for thee.

In King Lear, Act iii., Scene vi., Edgar says :—

Come o'er the bourn, Bessy, to me.

And the Fool :—

Her boat hath a leak,
And she must not speak
Why she dares not come over to thee.

So we presume there must have been an old English song with a somewhat similar burden.

CIX.

AYE WAKIN', OH.

Aye wakin' oh,
Wakin' aye and wearie,
Sleep I canna get,
For thinkin' o' my dearie.
When I sleep I dream,
When I wake I'm eerie;
Rest I canna get,
For thinkin' o' my dearie.

Ritson, in 1794, says that the above was 'dictated to him many years ago by a young gentleman, who had it from his grandfather.'

CX.

UP IN THE MORNING EARLY.

R. Burns.

Cauld blaws the wind frae east to west,
  The drift is driving sairly;
Sae loud and shrill's I hear the blast,
  I'm sure its winter fairly.

    Up in the morning's no for me
      Up in the morning early;
    When a' the hills are covered wi' snaw,
      I'm sure it's winter fairly!

The birds sit chittering in the thorn,
  A' day they fare but sparely;
And lang's the nicht frae e'en to morn—
  I'm sure it's winter fairly.

The chorus and tune of this song are very old.

CXI.

THE LAND O' THE LEAL.

    I'm wearin' awa' Jean,
    Like snaw when its thaw, Jean,
    I'm wearin' awa'
      To the land o' the leal.
    There's nae sorrow there, Jean,
    There's neither cauld nor care, Jean,
    The day is aye fair
      In the land o' the leal.

Our bonnie bairn's there, Jean,
She was baith gude and fair, Jean,
And oh ! we grudged her sair
  To the land o' the leal.
But sorrow's sel' wears past, Jean,
And joy is coming fast, Jean,
The joy that's aye to last
  In the land o' the leal.

Ye were aye leal and true, Jean,
Your task's ended now, Jean,
And I'll welcome you
  To the land o' the leal.
Now fare ye well, my ain Jean,
This warld's care is vain, Jean,
We'll meet and we'll be fain,
  In the land o' the leal.

Lady Nairne is essentially the authoress of this song ; but in its popular recitation it has been much altered, and, it seems to us, improved. It appeared soon after Burns's death, and was supposed to express his dying thoughts ; although in its original form there is no trace of such an intention on the part of the authoress.

CXII.

JOHN ANDERSON, MY JO.

R. Burns.

John Anderson, my jo, John,
  When we were first acquent,
Your locks were like the raven,
  Your bonnie brow was brent ;

But now your brow is beld, John,
   Your locks are like the snaw ;
But blessings on your frosty pow,
   John Anderson, my jo.

John Anderson, my jo, John,
   We clamb the hill thegither,
And mony a canty day, John,
   We've had wi' ane anither ;
Now we maun totter doun, John,
   But hand in hand we'll go,
And we'll sleep thegither at the foot,
   John Anderson, my jo.

Part II.

WILLIE BREW'D A PECK O' MAUT.

R. Burns.

O, Willie brew'd a peck o' maut,
  And Rab and Allan cam' to prie;
Three blyther lads, that lee lang night,
  We wadna fand in Christendie.

    We are na fou, we're no that fou,
      But just a wee drap in our e'e;
    The cock may craw, the day may daw,
      But aye we'll taste the barley bree.

Here are we met three merry boys;
  Three merry boys I trow are we:
And mony a nicht we've merry been,
  And mony mae we hope to be!

It is the mune—I ken her horn—
  That's blinkin' in the lift sae hie;
She shines sae bright to wyle us hame,
  But by my sooth she'll wait awee.

Wha first shall rise to gang awa',
  A cuckold coward loun is he;
Wha last beside his chair shall fa',
  He is the king amang us three.

The three "merry boys" were, Burns and his two
intimate friends, William Nicol and Allan Masterton, (both
masters in the Edinburgh High School). The latter
set the song to music.

CXIV.

TODLIN' HAME.

When I ha'e a saxpence under my thoom,
Then I get credit in ilka toun;
But aye when I'm puir they bid me gang by,
Oh, poverty parts gude company!
  Todlin' hame, todlin' hame,
  Couldna' my love come todlin' hame.

Fair fa' the gudewife, and send her gude sale;
She gi'es us white bannocks to relish her ale;
Syne, if that her tippeny chance to be sma',
We tak' a gude scour o't, and ca't awa.
  Todlin' him, todlin' hame,
  As round as a neep come todlin' hame.

My kimmer and I lay down to sleep,
Wi' twa pint-stoups at our bed feet;

And aye when we waken'd we drank them dry.
What think ye o' my wee kimmer and I?
  'Todlin' but, and todlin' ben,
  Sae round as my love comes todlin' hame.

Leeze me on liquor, my todlin' dow,
Ye're aye sae gude-humour'd when weetin' your
        mou'!
When sober sae sour, ye'll fecht wi' a flee,
That 'tis a blythe nicht to the bairns and me,
  When todlin' hame, todlin' hame,
  When, round as a neep, ye come todlin' hame.

"This is perhaps the first bottle-song that ever was
composed."—*Burns.*

CXV.

ANDRO' AND HIS CUTTY GUN.

Blythe, blythe, blythe was she,
  Blythe was she but and ben;
And weel she loo'd a Hawick gill,
  And leuch to see a tappit hen.
She took me in, and set me down,
  And hecht to keep me lawing-free;
But cunning carline that she was,
  She gart me birl my bawbee.

We loo'd the liquor well enough;
  But wae's my heart my cash was done,

Before that I had quench'd my drouth,
　And laith I was to pawn my shoon.
When we had three times toom'd our stoup.
　And the neist chappin new begun,
In started, to heeze up our hope,
　Young Andro' wi' his cutty gun.

The carline brought her kebbuck ben,
　With girdle-cakes weel toasted brown,
Weel does the canny kimmer ken
　They gar the swats gae glibber down.
We ca'd the bicker aft about ;
　Till dawning we ne'er jee'd our bun,
And aye the cleanest drinker out,
　Was Andro' wi' his cutty gun.

He did like ony mavis sing,
　And as I in his oxter sat,
He ca'd me ay his bonnie thing,
　And mony a sappy kiss I gat.
I hae been east, I hae been west,
　I hae been far ayont the sun ;
But the blythest lad that e'er I saw,
　Was Andro' wi' his cutty gun.

"*Andro' and his Cutty Gun* is the work of a master."—
Burns.

CXVI.

THE SOCIAL CUP.

Captain Charles Gray, R.M.

Blythe, blythe, and merry are we,
　Blythe are we, ane and a' ;

Aften ha'e we cantie been,
    But sic a nicht we never saw !

The gloamin saw us a' sit down,
    And meikle mirth has been our fa';
Then let the sang and toast gae roun'
    Till chanticleer begins to craw !
Blythe, blythe, and merry are we—
    Pick and wale o' merry men ;
What care we though the cock may craw,
    We're masters o' the tappit-hen ;

The auld kirk bell has chappit twal—
    Wha cares though she had chappit twa !
We're licht o' heart and winna part,
    Though time and tide may rin awa !
Blythe, blythe, and merry are we—
    Hearts that care can never ding ;
Then let time pass—we'll steal his glass,
    And pu' a feather frae his wing !

Now is the witching time of nicht,
    When ghaists, they say, are to be seen ;
And fays dance to the glow-worm's licht
    Wi' fairies in their gowns of green.
Blythe, blythe, and merry are we—
    Ghaists may tak' their midnight stroll ;
Witches ride on brooms astride,
    While we sit by the witchin' bowl !

Tut ! never speir how wears the morn—
    The moon's still blinkin' i' the sky,
And, gif like her we fill our horn,
    I dinna doubt we'll drink it dry !

Blythe, blythe, and merry are we—
    Blythe out-owre the barley bree ;
And let me tell, the moon hersel'
    Aft dips her toom horn i' the sea !

Then fill us up a social cup,
    And never mind the dapple-dawn ;
Just sit awhile—the sun may smile
    And licht us a' across the lawn !
Blythe, blythe, and merry are we ;—
    See ! the sun is keekin' ben ;
Gi'e time his glass—for months may pass
    Ere we ha'e sic a nicht again ;

This song was written in 1814.

CXVII.

THE DEIL'S AWA WI' TH' EXCISEMAN.

R. Burns.

The deil cam' fiddlin' through the toun,
    And danced awa' wi' th' exciseman ;
And ilka auld wife cries, Auld Mahoun,
    I wish you luck o' the prize man.

The deil's awa', the deil's awa',
    The deil's awa' wi' th' exciseman ;
He's danced awa', he's danced awa',
    He's danced awa' wi' th' exciseman !

We'll mak' our maut, and we'll brew our drink,
   We'll laugh, sing, and rejoice, man ;
And mony braw thanks to the meikle black deil,
   That danc'd awa' wi' th' exciseman.

There's threesome reels, there's foursome reels,
   There's hornpipes and strathspeys, man :
But the ae best dance e'er cam' to the land,
   Was, The deil's awa' wi' th' exciseman.

CXVIII.

CAULD KAIL IN ABERDEEN.

There's cauld kail in Aberdeen,
   And castocks in Stra'bogie,
Where ilka lad maun ha'e his lass,
   But I maun ha'e my cogie.
      For I maun ha'e my cogie, sirs,
         I canna want my cogie ;
      I wadna gi'e my three-gir'd cog
         For a' the wives in Bogie.

Johnny Smith has got a wife
   Wha scrimps him o' his cogie ;
But were she mine, upon my life,
   I'd dook her in a bogie.
      For I maun ha'e my cogie, sirs,
         I canna want my cogie ;
      I wadna gi'e my three-gir'd cog
         For a' the wives in Bogie.

Twa three todlin' weans they ha'e,
   The pride o' a' Stra'bogie ;

Whene'er the totums cry for meat,
  She curses aye his cogie;
    Crying, Wae betide the three-gir'd cog!
    Oh, wae betide the cogie;
    It does mair skaith than a' the ills
    That happen in Stra'bogie.

She fand him ance at Willie Sharp's;
  And, what they maist did laugh at,
She brak the bicker, spilt the drink,
  And tightly gouff'd his haffet;
    Crying, Wae betide the three-gir'd cog!
    Oh, wae betide the cogie,
    It does mair skaith than a' the ills
    That happen in Stra'bogie.

Yet here's to ilka honest soul
  Wha'll drink wi' me a cogie;
And for ilk silly whinging fool,
  We'll dook him in a bogie.
    For I maun ha'e my cogie, sirs,
    I canna want my cogie;
    I wadna gi'e my three-gir'd cog
    For a' the queans in Bogie.

Burns speaks of this as an old song; but the author is unknown.

CXIX.

NEIL GOW'S FAREWELL TO WHISKY.

Mrs. Lyon.—Born 1762; Died 1840.

You've surely heard o' famous Neil,
The man that play'd the fiddle weel;

I wat he was a canty cheil,
    And dearly lo'ed the whiskey, O !
And, aye sin he wore the tartan trews,
He dearly lo'ed the Athole brose ;
And wae was he, you may suppose.
    To play fareweel to whiskey, O.

Alake, quoth Neil, I'm frail and auld,
And find my blude grow unco cauld ;
I think 'twad make me blythe and bauld,
    A wee drap Highland whiskey, O.
Yet the doctors they do a' agree,
That whiskey's no the drink for me.
Saul ! quoth Neil, 'twill spoil my glee,
    Should they part me and whiskey, O.

Though I can baith get wine and ale,
And find my head and fingers hale,
I'll be content, though legs should fail,
    To play fareweel to whiskey, O.
But still I think on auld lang syne,
When Paradise our friends did tyne,
Because something ran 'in their mind,
    Forbid like Highland whiskey, O.

Come, a' ye powers o' music, come ;
I find my heart grows unco glum,
My fiddle-strings will no play bum,
    To say, Fareweel to whiskey, O.
Yet I'll take my fiddle in my hand,
And screw the pegs up while they'll stand ;
To make a lamentation grand,
    On gude auld Highland whiskey, O.

CXX.

TULLOCHGORUM.

Rev. J. Skinner.—Born, 1721; Died, 1807.

Come gie's a sang Montgomery cried,
And lay your disputes all aside,
What signifies't for folk to chide
 For what's been done before them?
Let Whig and Tory all agree,
Whig and Tory, Whig and Tory,
Let Whig and Tory all agree,
 To drop their Whig-mig-morum;
Let Whig and Tory all agree,
To spend the night in mirth and glee,
And cheerfu' sing, alang wi' me,
 The reel o' Tullochgorum.

O, Tullochgorum's my delight,
It gars us a' in ane unite,
And ony sumph that keeps up spite,
 In conscience I abhor him.
For blythe and cheery we's be a',
Blythe and cheery, blythe and cheery,
Blythe and cheery we's be a',
 And mak' a happy quorum.
For blythe and cheery we's be a',
As lang as we hae breath to draw,
And dance, till we be like to fa',
 The reel of Tullochgorum.

There needs na' be sae great a phrase,
Wi' dringing dull Italian lays,
I wadna gi'e our ain strathspeys
 For half a hundred score o' em.

They're douff and dowie at the best,
Douff and dowie, douff and dowie,
They're douff and dowie at the best
   Wi' a' their variorum.
They're douff and dowie at the best,
Their allegros and a' the rest,
They canna please a Scottish taste,
   Compar'd wi' Tullochgorum.

Let warldly minds themselves oppress
Wi' fears of want, and double cess,
And sullen sots themselves distress
   Wi' keeping up decorum :
Shall we sae sour and sulky sit,
Sour and sulky, sour and sulky,
Shall we sae sour and sulky sit,
   Like auld Philosophorum?
Shall we so sour and sulky sit,
Wi' neither sense, nor mirth, nor wit,
Nor ever rise to shake a fit
   To the reel of Tullochgorum?

May choicest blessings still attend
Each honest open-hearted friend,
And calm and quiet be his end,
   And a' that's good watch o'er him !
May peace and plenty be his lot,
Peace and plenty, peace and plenty,
May peace and plenty be his lot,
   And dainties a great store o' 'em ;
May peace and plenty be his lot,
Unstain'd by any vicious spot !
And may he never want a groat
   That's fond of Tullochgorum.

But for the dirty, yawning fool,
Who wants to be oppression's tool,
May envy gnaw his rotten soul,
    And discontent devour him !
May dool and sorrow be his chance,
Dool and sorrow, dool and sorrow,
May dool and sorrow be his chance,
    And nane say wae's me for 'im !
May dool and sorrow be his chance,
Wi' a' the ills that come frae France,
Whae'er he be, that winna dance
    The reel of Tullochgorum.

This is a good song ; but when Burns says it is 'the best that Scotland ever saw,' we may be allowed to repeat to ourselves, there is flattery in friendship.

CXXI.

TUNE YOUR FIDDLES.

John Skinner.

Tune your fiddles, tune them sweetly,
Play the marquis' reel discreetly,
Here we are a band completely,
    Fitted to be jolly.
Come, my boys, blythe and gawcie,
Every youngster choose his lassie,
Dance wi' life and be not saucy,
    Shy nor melancholy.

Lay aside your sour grimaces,
Clouded brows and drumlie faces,
Look about and see their Graces,
    How they smile delighted :

Now's the season to be merry,
Hang the thoughts of Charon's ferry,
Time enough to come camsterry,
    When we're auld and doited.

Butler, put about the claret,
Through us a' divide and share it,
Gordon Castle weel can spare it,
    It has claret plenty :
Wine's the true inspiring liquor,
Draffy drink may please the vicar,
When he grasps the foaming bicker,
    Vicars are not dainty.

We'll extol our noble master,
Sprung from many a brave ancestor,—
Heaven preserve him from disaster,
    So we pray in duty,
Prosper, too, our pretty duchess,
Safe from all distressful touches,
Keep her out of Pluto's clutches,
    Long in health and beauty.

Angels guard their gallant boy,
Make him long his father's joy,
Sturdy like the heir of Troy,
    Stout and brisk and healthy.
Pallas grant him every blessing,
Wit and strength, and size increasing,
Plutus, what's in thy possession,
    Make him rich and wealthy.

Youth, solace him with thy pleasure,
In refined and worthy measure :

Merit gain him choicest treasure,
      From the Royal donor:
Famous may he be in story,
Full of days and full of glory;
To the grave, when old and hoary,
      May he go with honour!

Gordons, join our hearty praises,
Honest, though in homely phrases,
Love our cheerful spirit raises,
      Lofty as the lark is:
Echo, waft our wishes daily,
Through the grove and through the alley;
Sound o'er every hill and valley,
      Blessings on our Marquis.

CXXII.

WILLIE WAS A WANTON WAG.

Willie was a wanton wag,
  The blythest lad that e'er I saw,
At bridals still he bore the brag,
  An' carried aye the gree awa'.
His doublet was of Zetland shag,
  And wow! but Willie he was braw,
And at his shoulder hung a tag,
  That pleased the lasses best of a'.

He was a man without a clag,
  His heart was frank without a flaw;
And aye whatever Willie said,
  It still was hauden as a law.

His boots they were made of the jag,
  When he went to the weaponschaw,
Upon the green nane durst him brag,
  The fiend a ane amang them a'.

And wasna Willie well worth gowd?
  He wan the love o' great and sma';
For after he the bride had kiss'd,
  He kiss'd the lasses hale sale a'.
Sae merrily round the ring they row'd,
  When by the hand he led them a',
And smack on smack on them bestowed,
  By virtue of a standing law.

And wasna Willie a great loon,
  As shyre a lick as e'er was seen?
When he danc'd wi' the lasses roun',
  The bridegroom speir'd where he had been.
Quoth Willie, I've been at the ring,
  Wi' bobbing baith my shanks are sair,
Gae ca' your bride and maidens in,
  For Willie he dow do nae mair.

Then rest ye, Willie, I'll gae out,
  And for a wee fill up the ring.
But, shame light on his souple snout,
  He wanted Willie's wanton fling.
Then straight he to the bride did fare,
  Says, Weels me on your bonnie face;
Wi' bobbing Willie's shanks are sair,
  And I'm come out to fill his place.

Bridegroom, she says, ye'll spoil the dance,
  And at the ring ye'll aye be lag,

Unless like Willie ye advance :
  O ! Willie has a wanton leg :
For wi't he learns us a' to steer,
  And foremost aye bears up the ring :
We will find nae sic dancing here,
  If we want Willie's wanton fling.

Mr. David Laing inclines to think that William Hamilton of Gilbertfield, (Born 1680?; Died **1751**), otherwise called " Wanton Willie," is the author as well as hero of this song.

CXXIII.

TRANENT WEDDING.

Peter Forbes.

It was at a wedding near Tranent,
Where scores an' scores on fun were bent,
An' to ride the broose wi' full intent,
  Was either nine or ten, jo !

    Then aff they a' set galloping, galloping,
    Legs an' arms a walloping, walloping,
    Shame take the hindmost, quo' Duncan
        M'Calpin,
    Laird o' Jelly Ben, jo.

The souter he was fidging fain,
An' stuck like roset till the mane,
'Till smash like auld boots in a drain,
  He nearly reach'd his end, jo !

The miller's mare flew o'er the souter.
An' syne began to glow'r about her,
Cries Hab, I'll gi'e ye double mouter,
 Gin ye'll ding Jelly Ben, jo.

Now Will the weaver rode sae kittle,
Ye'd thought he was a flying shuttle,
His doup it daddet like a bittle,
 But wafted till the end, jo.

The taylor had an awkward beast,
It funket first an' syne did reest,
Then threw poor snip five ell at least,
 Like auld breeks, o'er the mane, jo.

The blacksmith's beast was last of a',
Its sides like bellowses did blaw,
Till he an' it got sic a fa',
 An' bruises nine or ten, jo.

Now Duncan's mare she flew like drift,
And aye sae fast her feet did lift,
Between ilk stenn she ga'e a rift,
 Out frae her hinder end, jo.

Now Duncan's mare did bang them a',
To rin wi' him they manna fa',
Then up his grey mare he did draw,
 The broose it was his ain, jo.

Published in 1812. *Riding the Broose* is a noisy race
run by young men at country weddings, generally from
the bride's old home to that which is going to be her new.

The winner's prize is a kiss from the bride.   Burns says
of his *Auld Mare Maggie*,

> 'At Broose thou had ne'er a fellow
>   For pith and speed.'

CXXIV.

RATTLIN', ROARIN' WILLIE.

O rattlin', roarin' Willie,
  O he held to the fair.
And for to sell his fiddle,
  And buy some other ware ;
But parting wi' his fiddle,
  The saut tear blin't his ee ;
And rattlin', roarin' Willie,
  Ye're welcome hame to me.

O Willie, come sell your fiddle,
  O sell your fiddle sae fine ;
O Willie come sell your fiddle,
  And buy a pint o' wine.
If I should sell my fiddle,
  The warl' wad think I was mad ;
For mony a rantin' day,
  My fiddle and I hae had.

As I cam' by Crochallan,
  I cannily keekit ben ;
Rattlin', roarin' Willie,
  Was sitting at yon board-en'.

Sitting at yon board-en',
  And amang gude companie ;
Rattlin', roarin' Willie,
  Ye're welcome hame to me?

Burns added the last verse to this old song.

CXXV.

BRIDEKIRK'S HUNTING.

Adam Carlyle.

The cock's at the crawing,
The day's at the dawing,
The cock's at the crawing,
  We're o'er lang here.

    Bridekirk's hunting,
    Bridekirk's hunting,
    Bridekirk's hunting
    'S the morn, an' it be fair.

There's Bridekirk and Brackenwhat,
Limekilns and Murraywhat,
Daltonhook and Dormont,
  An' a' shall be there.

Daltonhook and Dormont,
Aye our Lord Stormont,
Aye our Lord Stormont,
  An' a' shall be there.

Ah, sic' a yumphing,
Ah, sic' a yumphing,
Ah, sic' a yumphing,
    About the little hare.

There's Gingler and Jowler,
Tingler and Towler,
Proudfit and Bawtie,
    And a' shall be there.

Thy dog and my dog,
My dog and thy dog,
Thy dog and my dog,
    About the little hare.

Fie rin Mopsey,
Fie rin Cropsey,
Fie rin Mopsey,
    Or Cropsey 'll hae the hare.

Up and down yon bonnie lea,
Up and down yon bonnie lea,
Up and down yon bonnie lea,
    The hun's 'll hae the hare.

The author of this song, the Laird of Bridekirk, was a well-known man in Annandale, Dumfriesshire. Carlyle of Inveresk,* speaks of him as a kinsman. Fifty or sixty years ago, there were many traditions of his exploits, current in that region, amongst others that on one hunting occasion his voice had been heard from 'Woodcockair to Wintrop Head',—a distance of ten miles as the crow flies ! He was a Whig; and as he took no pains to

* *Autobiography of the Rev. Alexander Carlyle.* (Edin., 1859), p. 23.

conceal his feelings, he was seized, on the highway near his own house, by the Pretender's army, in 1745, on its retreat from Carlisle. In passing through Dumfries, as their prisoner, he made himself conspicuous at the officers' mess by obstinately refusing to give any sign when Prince Charlie's health was drunk. When the enthusiasm had subsided a little, however, he stood up alone, and drank, "Confusion to the Pretender."

CXXVI.

FOR A' THAT AND A' THAT.

R. Burns.

Is there, for honest poverty,
  That hangs his head and a' that?
The coward-slave, we pass him by
  We dare be poor for a' that!
For a' that, and a' that,
  Our toils obscure, and a' that;
The rank is but the guinea's stamp,
  The man's the gowd for a' that.

What tho' on hamely fare we dine,
  Wear hoddin gray, and a' that;
Gie fools their silks, and knaves their wine,
  A man's a man for a' that:
For a' that, an' a' that,
  Their tinsel show, and a' that;
The honest man, though e'er sae poor,
  Is king o' men, for a' that.

Ye see yon birkie, ca'd a lord,
  Wha struts, and stares, and a' that;
Tho' hundreds worship at his word.
  He's but a coof, for a' that.

For a' that, and a' that,
   His riband, star, and a' that.
The man of independent mind,
   He looks and laughs at a' that.

A prince can make a belted knight,
   A marquis, duke, and a' that ;
But an honest man's aboon his might,
   Guid faith, he mauna fa' that !
For a' that, and a' that,
   Their dignities, and a' that,
The pith o' sense, and pride o' worth,
   Are higher ranks than a' that.

Then let us pray, that come it may,
   As come it will, for a' that,
That sense and worth, o'er a' the earth,
   May bear the gree, and a' that,
For a' that, and a' that,
   It's comin' yet, for a' that,
That man to man, the warld o'er,
   Shall brothers be, for a' that.

CXXVII.

TARRY WOO'.

Tarry woo', tarry woo',
   Tarry woo' is ill to spin ;
Card it weil, card it weil,
   Card it weil, ere ye begin.

When it's cardit, row'd, and spun,
Then the wark is haflins done ;
But when woven, dress'd, and clean,
It may be cleadin' for a queen.

Sing my bonnie harmless sheep,
That feed upon the mountains steep,
Bleating sweetly, as ye go
Through the winter's frost and snow.
Hart, and hynd, and fallow-deer,
Not by half sae useful are,
Frae kings, to him that hauds the plou',
All are obliged to tarry woo'.

Up, ye shepherds, dance and skip ;
Ower the hills and valleys trip ;
Sing up the praise of tarry woo',
Sing the flocks that bear it too ;
Harmless creatures, without blame,
That clead the back, and cram the wame ;
Keep us warm and hearty fou';
Leeze me on the tarry woo'.

How happy is the shepherd's life,
Far frae courts and free of strife !
While the gimmers bleat and bae,
And the lambkins answer mae ;
No such music to his ear !
Of thief or fox he has no fear ;
Sturdy kent and collie true,
Weil defend the tarry woo'.

He lives content and envies none ;
Not even the monarch on his throne,

Tho' he the royal sceptre sways,
Has such pleasant holidays.
Who'd be king, can ony tell,
When a shepherd sings sae well?
Sings sae well, and pays his due
With honest heart and tarry woo'!

From the *Tea-Table Miscellany.* ' A very pretty song ;
but I fancy that the first half stanza, as well as the tune
itself, is much older than the rest of the words'.—*Burns.*

CXXVIII.

JOHN OF BADENYON.

Rev. John Skinner.

When first I came to be a man of twenty years
    or so,
I thought myself a handsome youth, and fain
    the world would know ;
In best attire I stept abroad, with spirits brisk and
    gay ;
And here, and there, and everywhere, was like a
    morn in May.
No care I had, no fear of want, but rambled up
    and down ;
And for a beau I might have pass'd in country
    or in town :
I still was pleased where'er I went ; and, when
    I was alone,
I tuned my pipe, and pleased myself wi' John
    of Badenyon.

Now in the days of youthful prime a mistress I
    must find ;
For love, they say, gives one an air, and ev'n
    improves the mind :
On Phillis fair, above the rest, kind fortune
    fix'd my eyes ;
Her piercing beauty struck my heart and she
    became my choice :
To Cupid, then, with hearty prayer, I offer'd
    many a vow,
And danced and sung, and sigh'd and swore, as
    other lovers do ;
But when at last I breathed my flame, I found
    her cold as stone ;
I left the girl, and tuned my pipe to John of
    Badenyon.

When love had thus my heart beguiled with
    foolish hopes and vain,
To friendship's port I steer'd my course, and
    laugh'd at lovers' pain ;
A friend I got, by lucky chance, 'twas something
    like divine ;
An honest friend's a precious gift, and such a
    gift was mine.
And now, whatever might betide, a happy man
    was I,
In any strait I knew to whom I freely might
    apply.
A strait soon came ; my friend I tried, he laugh'd,
    and spurn'd my moan ;
I hied me home, and pleased myself with John
    of Badenyon.

I thought I would be wiser next, and would a
     patriot turn,
Began to doat on Johnie Wilkes, and cry'd up
     parson Horne ;
Their noble spirit I admir'd, and praised their
     noble zeal,
Who had, with flaming tongue and pen, maintain'd
     the public weal.
But, e'er a month or two had pass'd, I found
     myself betray'd ;
'Twas Self and Party, after all, for all the stir
     they made.
At last I saw these factious knaves insult the
     very throne ;
I cursed them all, and tuned my pipe to John of
     Badenyon.

What next to do I mused a while, still hoping
     to succeed ;
I pitch'd on books for company, and gravely
     tried to read ;
I bought and borrowed every where, and studied
     night and day,
Nor miss'd what dean or doctor wrote, that
     happen'd in my way.
Philosophy I now esteem'd the ornament of
     youth,
And carefully, through many a page, I hunted
     after truth :
A thousand various schemes I tried, and yet
     was pleased with none ;
I threw them by, and tuned my pipe to John
     of Badenyon.

And now, ye youngsters everywhere, who wish
        to make a show,
Take heed in time, nor vainly hope for happiness
        below ;
What you may fancy pleasure here is but an
        empty name ;
And girls, and friends, and books also, you'll
        find them all the same.
Then be advised, and warning take from such
        a man as me ;
I'm neither pope nor cardinal, nor one of high
        degree ;
You'll meet displeasure every where ; then do
        as I have done—
But tune your pipe and please yourself with John
        of Badenyon.

"This excellent song is the composition of my worthy
friend, old Skinner, at Linshart."—*Burns.*

Pity that Burns, who saw the excellence of this patri-
archal song, had not told us the meaning of *John of
Badenyon !*

CXXIX.

AULD LANG SYNE.

R. Burns.

Should auld acquaintance be forgot,
    And never brought to min'?
Should auld acquaintance be forgot,
    And days o' lang syne?

      For auld lang syne, my dear,
        For auld lang syne,
      We'll tak' a cup o' kindness yet,
        For auld lang syne.

We twa ha'e run about the braes,
   And pu'd the gowans fine ;
But we've wander'd mony a weary foot,
   Sin' auld lang syne.

We twa ha'e paid'lt in the burn,
   Frae mornin' sun till dine :
But seas between us braid ha'e roar'd,
   Sin' auld lang syne.

And here's a hand, my trusty fiere,
   And gi'e's a hand o' thine ;
And we'll tak' a richt gude-willie waught,
   For auld lang syne.

And surely ye'll be your pint-stoup,
   And surely I'll be mine ;
And we'll tak' a cup o' kindness yet,
   For auld lang syne.

There are several versions of *Auld Lang Syne;* but
this of Burns has now deservedly got complete possession
of the tune.

CXXX.

GOOD NIGHT AND JOY BE WI' YOU A'.

Sir Alexander Boswell.

Good night, and joy be wi' ye a'
   Your harmless mirth has cheered my heart :
May life's fell blast out o'er ye blaw !
   In sorrow may ye never part !

My spirit lives, but strength is gone ;
  The mountain-fires now blaze in vain :
Remember, sons, the deeds I've done,
  And in your deeds I'll live again !

When on yon muir our gallant clan
  Frae boasting faes their banners tore,
Wha showed himself a better man,
  Or fiercer wav'd the red claymore ?
But when in peace—then mark me there,
  When through the glen the wand'rer came
I gave him of our hardy fare,
  I gave him here a welcome hame.

The auld will speak, the young maun hear ;
  Be canty, but be good and leal ;
Your ain ills aye ha'e heart to bear,
  Anither's aye ha'e heart to feel.
So, ere I set, I'll see you shine,
  I'll see you triumph ere I fa' ;
My parting breath shall boast you mine,
  Good night, and joy be wi' ye a'.

CXXXI.

MY HEART'S IN THE HIGHLANDS.

R. Burns.

My heart's in the Highlands, my heart is not here ;
My heart's in the Highlands, a-chasing the deer ;
Chasing the wild deer, and following the roe ;
My heart's in the Highlands wherever I go.

Farewell to the Highlands, farewell to the north,
The birth-place of valour, the country of worth ;
Wherever I wander, wherever I rove,
The hills of the Highlands for ever I love.

Farewell to the mountains high-cover'd with snow ;
Farewell to the straths and green valleys below ;
Farewell to the forests and wild-hanging woods ;
Farewell to the torrents and loud-pouring floods.
My heart's in the Highlands, my heart is not here ;
My heart's in the Highlands a-chasing the deer ;
Chasing the wild deer, and following the roe,
My heart's in the Highlands wherever I go.

The first four lines of this song are from a distracted
old Scotch-Irish ballad.

CXXXII.

A WET SHEET

Allan Cunningham.—Born 1785 ; Died 1842.

A wet sheet and a flowing sea,
  A wind that follows fast,
And fills the white and rustling sail,
  And bends the gallant mast ;
And bends the gallant mast, my boys,
  While, like the eagle free,
Away the good ship flies, and leaves
  Old England on the lee.

Oh for a soft and gentle wind !
  I heard a fair one cry ;
But give to me the swelling breeze,
  And white waves heaving high ;
The white waves heaving high, my boys,
  The good ship tight and free—
The world of waters is our home,
  And merry men are we.

There's tempest in yon horned moon
  And lightning in yon cloud ;
And hark the music, mariners,
  The wind is piping loud ;
The wind is piping loud, my boys,
  The lightning flashes free—
The hollow oak our palace is,
  Our heritage the sea.

CXXXIII.

THE EMIGRANT'S FAREWELL.

Thomas Pringle.—Born 1789 ; Died 1834.

Our native land, our native vale,
  A long and last adieu !
Farewell to bonny Teviotdale,
  And Cheviot mountains blue !

Farewell, ye hills of glorious deeds,
  And streams renown'd in song ;
Farewell, ye braes and blossom'd meads
  Our hearts have lov'd so long.

Farewell the blythesome broomy knowes
 Where thyme and harebells grow ;
Farewell the hoary, haunted howes,
 O'erhung with birk and sloe !

The mossy cave and mouldering tower
 That skirt our native dell ;
The martyr's grave, and lover's bower,
 We bid a sad farewell !

Home of our love ! our fathers' home,
 Land of the brave and free !
The sail is flapping on the foam
 That bears us far from thee !

We seek a wild and distant shore,
 Beyond the western main :
We leave thee to return no more,
 Nor view thy cliffs again !

Our native land, our native vale,
 A long, a last adieu !
Farewell to bonny Teviotdale,
 And Scotland's mountains blue.

Part III.

THE GABERLUNZIE MAN.

Attributed to James V.—Born 1512; Died 1542.

The pawky auld carle came o'er the lea,
Wi' mony gude e'ens and days to me,
Saying, Gudewife, for your courtesie,
   Will you lodge a silly puir man?
The nicht was cauld, the carl was wat.
And down ayont the ingle he sat;
My dochter's shoulders he 'gan to clap,
   And cadgily ranted and sang.

O wow! quo' he, were I as free,
As first when I saw this countrie,
How blythe and merry wad I be!
   And I wad never think lang.
He canty grew, and she grew fain;
But little did her auld minny ken,
What thir slee twa together were sayin',
   When wooing they were sae thrang.

And O ! quo' he, an ye were as black
As e'er the crown of my daddy's hat,
'Tis I wad lay thee by my back,
    And awa' wi' me thou should gang.
And O ! quo' she, an' I were as white,
As e'er the snaw lay on the dike,
I'd cleed me braw and lady like,
    And awa wi' thee I'd gang.

Between the twa was made a plot,
They raise a wee before the cock,
And wilily they shot the lock,
    And fast to the bent are they gane.
Up the morn the auld wife raise
And at her leisure put on her claise ;
Syne to the servant's bed she gaes.
    To speer for the silly poor man.

She gaed to the bed where the beggar lay,
The strae was cauld, he was away,
She clapt her hands, cried, Waladay,
    For some of our gear will be gane.
Some ran to coffer, and some to kist,
But nought was stoun that could be miss'd ;
She danced her lane, cried, Praise be blest,
    I have lodged a leal poor man.

Since naething's awa', as we can learn,
The kirn's to kirn, and milk to earn,
Gae butt the house, lass, and wauken my bairn,
    And bid her come quickly ben.
The servant gaed where the dochter lay,
The sheets were cauld, she was away,

And fast to the gudewife 'gan say
  She's aff wi' the gaberlunzie-man.

O fy gar ride, and fy gar rin,
And haste ye find these traytors again;
For she's be burnt, and he's be slain,
  The wearifu' gaberlunzie-man.
Some rode upo' horse, some ran a-fit,
The wife was wud, and out o' her wit:
She couldna gang, nor yet could she sit
  But aye she cursed and she bann'd.

Meantime far hind out o'er the lea
Fu' snug in a glen where nane could see.
The twa, with kindly sport and glee,
  Cut frae a new cheese a whang:
The priving was good, it pleased them baith,
To lo'e her for aye, he ga'e her his aith;
Quo' she, to leave thee I will be laith,
  My winsome gaberlunzie-man.

O kenn'd my minny I were wi' you,
I'll-far'dly wad she crook her mou',
Sic a poor man she'd never trow,
  After the gaberlunzie-man.
My dear, quo' he, ye're yet o'er young.
And haena learn'd the beggars' tongue,
To follow me frae toun to toun,
  And carry the gaberlunzie on.

Wi' cauk and keel I'll win your bread,
And spindles and whorles for them wha need,
Whilk is a gentle trade indeed,
  To carry the gaberlunzie on.

I'll bow my leg, and crook my knee,
And draw a black clout o'er my e'e,
A cripple or blind they will ca' me,
    While we shall be merry and sing.

CXXXV.

MY JO JANET.

Sweet sir, for your courtesie,
    When ye come by the Bass, then,
For the love ye bear to me,
    Buy me a keekin'-glass, then.
Keek into the draw-well,
        Janet, Janet;
There ye'll see your bonnie sel',
        My jo Janet.

Keekin' in the draw-well clear,
    What if I fa' in, sir?
Then a' my kin will say and swear
    I droun'd mysel' for sin, sir.
Haud the better by the brae,
        Janet, Janet;
Haud the better by the brae,
        My jo Janet.

Gude sir, for your courtesie,
    Coming through Aberdeen, then,
For the love ye bear to me,
    Buy me a pair o' shoon, then.

Clout the auld, the new are dear,
    Janet, Janet;
Ae pair may gain ye half a year,
    My jo Janet.

But what if dancing on the green,
    And skippin' like a maukin,
They should see my clouted shoon,
    Of me they will be talkin'.
Dance aye laigh, and late at e'en,
    Janet, Janet;
Syne a' their fau'ts will no be seen,
    My jo Janet

Kind sir, for your courtesie,
    When ye gae to the cross, then,
For the love ye bear to me,
    Buy me a pacin'-horse, then.
Pace upon your spinnin'-wheel,
    Janet, Janet;
Pace upon your spinnin'-wheel,
    My jo Janet.

My spinnin'-wheel is auld and stiff,
    The rock o't winna stand, sir;
To keep the temper-pin in tiff,
    Employs richt aft my hand, sir.
Mak' the best o't that ye can,
    Janet, Janet;
But like it never wale a man,
    My jo Janet.

M

CXXXVI.

SCORNFU' NANCY.

Nancy's to the green-wood gane,
  To hear the gowdspink chatt'ring :
And Willie he has follow'd her,
  To gain her love by flatt'ring :
But a' that he could say or do,
  She geck'd and scorned at him :
And aye when he began to woo
  She bid him mind wha' gat him.

What ails ye at my dad, quoth he,
  My minny or my aunty?
With crowdy-mowdy they fed me,
  Lang-kail and ranty-tanty :
With bannocks of good barley-meal,
  Of thae there was right plenty,
With chappit stocks fu' butter'd weel ;
  And was not that right dainty?

Altho' my father was nae laird
  ('Tis daffin to be vaunty),
He keepit aye a good kail-yard,
  A ha' house and a pantry :
A good blue bonnet on his head,
  An owrlay 'bout his craigy ;
And aye, until the day he died,
  He rade on good shanks-nagy.

Now wae and wonder on your snout,
  Wad ye hae bonny Nancy?

Wad ye compare yoursel' to me,
  A docken till a tansy?
I have a wooer o' my ain,
  They ca' him souple Sandy,
And well I wat, his bonny mou'
  Is sweet like sugar-candy.

Now Nancy, what needs a' this din?
  Do I not ken this Sandy?
I'm sure the chief of a' his kin
  Was Rab the beggar randy :
His minny, Meg, upo' her back,
  Bare baith him and his billy ;
Will ye compare a nasty pack
  To me your winsome Willy?

My gutcher left a good braid sword ;
  'Tho' it be auld and rusty,
Yet ye may tak' it on my word,
  It is baith stout and trusty ;
And if I can but get it drawn,
  Which will be right uneasy,
I shall lay baith my lugs in pawn,
  'That he shall get a heezy.

Then Nancy turn'd her round about,
  And said, Did Sandy hear ye,
Ye wadna' miss to get a clout ;
  I ken he disna' fear ye :
Sae haud your tongue, and say nae mair,
  Set somewhere else your fancy ;
For as lang's Sandy's to the fore
  Ye never shall get Nancy.

This is supposed to be a very old song, and to have come down to us without mutilation.

CXXXVII.

JOCKY SAID TO JENNY.

Jocky said to Jenny, Jenny, wilt thou do't?
Ne'er a fit, quo' Jenny, for my tocher good;
For my tocher good, I winna marry thee.
E'en's ye like, quo' Jocky; ye may let it be !

I ha'e gowd and gear, I ha'e land eneugh,
I ha'e seven good owsen gangin' in a pleugh,
Gangin' in a pleugh, and linkin' ower the lea :
And gin ye winna tak' me, I can let ye be.

I ha'e a gude ha' house, a barn, and a byre,
A stack afore the door, I'll mak' a rantin fire :
I'll mak' a rantin fire, and merry shall we be :
And, gin ye winna tak' me, I can let ye be.

Jenny said to Jocky, Gin ye winna tell,
Ye shall be the lad ; I'll be the lass mysel' :
Ye're a bonnie lad, and I'm a lassie free ;
Ye're welcomer to tak' me than to let me be.

CXXXVIII.

DUNCAN GRAY.

R. Burns.

Duncan Gray cam' here to woo,
 Ha, ha, the wooing o't,
On blythe Yule nicht, when we were fou,
 Ha, ha, the wooing o't ;

Maggie coost her head fu' high,
Look'd asklent, and unco sleigh,
Gart puir Duncan stand abeigh,
    Ha, ha, the wooing o't.

Duncan fleech'd, and Duncan pray'd,
    Ha, ha, the wooing o't;
Meg was deaf as Ailsa Craig,
    Ha, ha, the wooing o't.
Duncan sigh'd baith out and in,
Grat his e'en baith bleert and blin',
Spak' o' louping o'er a linn;
    Ha, ha, the wooing o't.

Time and chance are but a tide,
    Ha, ha, the wooing o't;
Slighted love is sair to bide,
    Ha, ha, the wooing o't.
Shall I, like a fool, quoth he,
For a haughty hizzie die?
She may gae to—France for me!
    Ha, ha, the wooing o't.

How it comes, let doctors tell,
    Ha, ha, the wooing o't;
Meg grew sick, as he grew hale,
    Ha, ha, the wooing o't.
Something in her bosom wrings,
For relief a sigh she brings;
And O, her e'en they spak' sic things!
    Ha, ha, the wooing o't.

Duncan was a lad o' grace,
    Ha, ha, the wooing o't;

Maggie's was a piteous case,
　　Ha, ha, the wooing o't.
Duncan couldna' be her death,
Swelling pity smoor'd his wrath;
Now they're crouse and canty baith,
　　Ha, ha, the wooing o't.

CXXXIX.

JOCK O' HAZELDEAN

Sir Walter Scott, Bart.—Born 1771; Died 1832.

" Why weep ye by the tide, ladye,
　　Why weep ye by the tide?
I'll wed ye to my youngest son,
　　And ye shall be his bride;
And ye shall be his bride, ladye,
　　Sae comely to be seen:"
But aye she loot the tears down fa',
　　For Jock o' Hazeldean.

" Now let this wilful grief be done,
　　And dry that cheek so pale:
Young Frank is chief of Errington,
　　And Lord of Langley-dale;
His step is first in peaceful ha',
　　His sword in battle keen:"
But aye she loot the tears down fa',
　　For Jock o' Hazeldean.

" A chain o' gold ye sall not lack,
　　Nor braid to bind your hair,
Nor mettled hound, nor managed hawk,
　　Nor palfrey fresh and fair:

And you, the foremost o' them a',
   Shall ride, our forest queen :"
But aye she loot the tears down fa',
   For Jock o' Hazeldean.

The kirk was deck'd at morning-tide,
   The tapers glimmered fair ;
The priest and bridegroom wait the bride
   And dame and knight were there :
They sought her baith by bower and ha' :
   The ladye was not seen !
She's o'er the border, and awa,
   Wi' Jock o' Hazeldean.

CXL.

ROY'S WIFE.

Mrs. Grant, of Carron.—Born 1745 ; Died 1814 ?

Roy's wife of Alldivalloch,
   Roy's wife of Alldivalloch,
Wat ye how she cheated me,
   As I cam' o'er the Braes o' Balloch.

She vow'd, she swore, she wad be mine,
   She said she lo'ed me best o' ony ;
But oh ! the fickle, faithless quean,
   She's ta'en the carle, and left her Johnnie.

O, she was a canty quean,
   We'el could she dance the Hielan' walloch :
How happy I, had she been mine,
   Or I been Roy of Alldivalloch !

Her face sae fair, her e'en sae clear,
 Her wee bit mou' sae sweet an' bonnie;
To me she ever will be dear,
 Though she's forever left her Johnnie.

CXLI.

THE RUNAWAY BRIDE.

A laddie and a lassie,
 Dwelt in the south countrie;
They ha'e coost their claes thegither,
 And wedded they wad be:
On Tuesday to the bridal feast
 Cam fiddlers flocking free;
But hey play up the rinaway bride,
 For she has ta'en the gee.

She had nae run a mile or mair,
 Till she 'gan to consider
The angering of her father dear,
 The vexing of her mither;
The slighting of the silly bridegroom,
 The warst of a' the three;
Then hey play up the rinaway bride,
 For she has ta'en the gee.

Her father and her mither baith
 Ran after her wi' speed;
And aye they ran until they came,
 Unto the water of Tweed:

And when they came to Kelso town,
 They gar't the clap gang through;

Saw ye a lass wi' a hood and mantle,
 The face o't lined up wi' blue,
The face o't lined up wi' blue,
 And the tail lin'd up wi' green ;
Saw ye a lass wi' a hood and mantle,
 Should ha'e been married on Tuesday't ee'n ?

CXLII.

SLICHTIT NANCY.

'Tis I ha'e seven braw new gowns,
 And ither seven better to mak' ;
And yet, for a' my new gowns,
 My wooer has turn'd his back.
Besides, I have seven milk-kye.
 And Sandy he has but three ;
And yet, for a' my gude kye,
 The laddie winna ha'e me.

My daddy's a delver of dikes,
 My mother can card and spin,
And I'm a fine fodgel lass,
 And the siller comes linkin' in.
The siller comes linkin' in,
 And it's fu' fair to see ;
And fifty times wow ! O wow !
 What ails the lads at me ?

Whenever our Bawty does bark,
 Then fast to the door I rin,
To see gin ony young spark,
 Will light and venture in :

But ne'er a ane will come in,
  Tho' mony a ane gaes by,
Sine far ben the house I rin ;
  And a weary wight am I.

When I was at my first prayers,
  I pray'd but ance i' the year,
I wish'd for a handsome young lad,
  And a lad wi' muckle gear.
When I was at my neist prayers,
  I pray'd but now and than,
I fash'd na my head about gear,
  If I got a handsome young man.

Now I am at my last prayers,
  I pray on baith nicht and day,
And, oh. if a beggar wad come,
  With that same beggar I'd gae.
And, oh, and what 'll come o' me !
  And, oh, and what will I do !
That sic a braw lassie as I
  Should die for a wooer, I trow !

We believe this song to be much older than Ramsay's
time ; probably he added to it.   It was printed first in
his *Tea Table Miscellany.*

CXLIII.

HEY, HOW, MY JOHNIE LAD.

Hey, how, my Johnie lad,
  Ye're no sae kind's ye should ha'e been.
For gin your voice I hadna kent,
  I'm sure I couldna trust my een :

Sae weel's ye might ha'e courted me,
  Sae sweetly 'courted me' bedeen ;
Hey, how, my Johnie lad,
  Ye're no sae kind's ye should ha'e been.

My father, he was at the pleugh,
  My mither, she was at the mill ;
My billie, he was at the moss,
  And no ane near our sport to spill ;
The feint a body was there in,
  Ye needna fley'd for being seen.
Hey, how, my Johnie lad,
  Ye're no sae kind's ye should ha'e been.

But I maun ha'e anither joe,
  Whase love gangs never out o' mind,
And winna let the moment pass
  When to a lass he can be kind :
Then gang ye're ways to blinking Bess,
  Nae mair for Johnie shall she grean :
Hey, how, my Johnie lad,
  Ye're no sae kind's ye should ha'e been.

From Herd's Collection, 1776.

CXLIV.

THE YELLOW-HAIR'D LADDIE.

The yellow-hair'd laddie sat doun on yon brae,
Cried, Milk the yowes, lassie, let nane o' them
    gae ;

And aye as she milkit, she merrily sang,
The yellow-hair'd laddie shall be my gudeman.
  And aye as she milkit, she merrily sang,
   The yellow-hair'd laddie shall be my gudeman.

The weather is cauld, and my cleadin is thin,
The yowes are new clipt, and they winna bucht
     in;
They winna bucht in, although I should dee:
Oh, yellow-hair'd laddie, be kind unto me.

The gudewife cries butt the house, Jennie, come
     ben;
The cheese is to mak', and the butter's to kirn.
Though butter, and cheese, and a' should gang
     sour,
I'll crack and I'll kiss wi' my love ae half-hour.
  It's ae lang half-hour, and we'll e'en mak' it
    three,
  For the yellow-hair'd laddie my gudeman shall
    be.

Printed by Ramsay as an old song.

CXLV.

COLIN CLOUT.

Chanticleer, wi' noisy whistle,
  Bids the housewife rise in haste,
Colin Clout begins to hirsle,
  Slawly frae his sleepless nest,

Love that raises sic a clamour.
　Drivin' lads and lassies mad ;
Wae's my heart ! had coost his glamour,
　O'er poor Colin, luckless lad.

Cruel Jenny, lack a daisy !
　Lang had gart him greet and grane,
Colin's pate was haflins crazy,
　Jenny laughed at Colin's pain.
Slawly, up his duds he gathers,
　Slawly, slawly trudges out,
An' frae the fauld he drives his wedders,
　Happier far than Colin Clout.

Now the sun, rais'd frae his nappie,
　Set the orient in a lowe,
Drinkin' ilka glancin' drappie,
　I' the field, an' i' the knowe.
Mony a birdie, sweetly singin',
　Flaffer'd briskly round about ;
An' monie a daintie flowerie springin',
　A' were blythe but Colin Clout.

What is this? cries Colin glow'rin',
　Glaiked-like, a' round about,
Jenny ! this is past endurin' :
　Death man ease poor Colin Clout.
A' the night I toss and tumble,
　Never can I close an e'e,
A' the day I grane an' grumble,
　Jenny, this is a' for thee.

Ye'll ha'e nane but farmer Patie,
　'Cause the fallow's rich, I trow,

Aiblins though he shouldna cheat ye,
  Jenny, ye'll ha'e cause to rue.
Auld, and gleed, and crooked-backed,—
  Siller bought at sic a price,—
Ah, Jenny ! gin you lout to tak' it,
  Folk will say ye're no o'er nice.

Fragment of an old song ; the rest is supposed to be lost.

CXLVI.

YOUNG JOCKEY.

R. Burns.

Young Jockey was the blythest lad,
  In a' our town and here awa' ;
Fu' blythe he whistled at the gaud,
  Fu' lichtly danced he in the ha' !
He roosed my een sae bonnie blue,
  He roosed my waist sae genty sma' ;
And aye my heart cam' to my mou',
  When ne'er a body heard or saw.

My Jockey toils upon the plain,
  Thro' wind and weet, thro' frost and snaw ;
And ower the lee I look fu' fain,
  When Jockey's owsen hameward ca'.
And aye the nicht comes round again,
  When in his arms he taks me a',
And aye he vows he'll be my ain
  As lang as he has breath to draw.

CXLVII.

MY COLLIER LADDIE

Whar live ye, my bonnie lass,
    And tell me what they ca' ye?
My name, she says, is Mistress Jean,
    And I follow the collier laddie.

See ye not yon hills and dales,
    The sun shines on sae brawlie!
They a' are mine, and they shall be thine
    Gin ye leave your collier laddie.

Ye shall gang in gay attire,
    Weel buskit up sae gawdy;
And ane to wait on every hand,
    Gin ye leave your collier laddie.

Though you had a' the sun shines on,
    And the earth conceals sae lowly,
I wad turn my back on you and it a',
    And embrace my collier laddie.

I can win my five-pennies in a day,
    And spen't at nicht fu' brawlie;
And make my bed in the collier's neuk,
    And lie down wi' my collier laddie.

Love for love is the bargain for me,
    Tho' the wee cot-house should haud me,
And the warld before me to win my bread,
    And fair fa' my collier laddie.

' I do not know a blyther old song than this.'—*Burns.*

CXLVIII.

LOW DOWN IN THE BROOM.

My daddie is a cankert carle,
  He'll no twin wi' his gear :
My minnie she's a scauldin' wife,
  Hauds a' the house asteer.

    But let them say, or let them do,
      It's a' ane to me,
    For he's low doun, he's in the broom,
      That's waiting on me :
    Waiting on me, my love,
      He's waitin' on me,
    For he's low doun, he's in the broom,
      That's waitin' on me.

My auntie Kate sits at her wheel,
  And sair she lightlies me ;
But weel I ken it's a' envy,
  For ne'er a joe has she.

My cousin Kate was sair beguiled
  Wi' Johnnie o' the Glen ;
And aye sinsyne she cries, Beware
  Of fause deluding men.

Gleed Sandy he cam' wast yestreen,
  And speir'd when I saw Pate ;
And aye sinsyne the neebors round
  They jeer me air and late.

But let them say, or let them do,
    It's a' ane to me,
For he's low doun, he's in the broom,
    That's waiting on me;
Waiting on me, my love,
    He's waiting on me,
For he's low doun, he's in the broom,
    That's waiting on me.

CXLIX.

ETTRICK BANKS.

On Ettrick banks, on a simmer's night,
    At gloamin' when the sheep drave hame,
I met my lassie braw and tight,
    Come wading, bare-foot, a' her lane.
My heart grew licht, I ran, I flang
    My arms about her lily neck,
And kiss'd and clapp'd her there fu' lang,
    My words they were na monie feck.

I said, My lassie, will ye gang
    To the Highland hills the Erse* to learn
I'll gie thee baith a cow and ewe,
    When ye come to the brig o' Earn.
At Leith auld meal comes in, ne'er fash,
    And herrings at the Broomielaw,
Cheer up your heart, my bonnie lass,
    There's gear to win ye never saw.

* *Erysche*, or Gaelic, the language of the Highlands.

All day when we ha'e wrought eneuch,
　When winter frosts and snaw begin,
Soon as the sun gaes west the loch,
　At night when ye sit down to spin,
I'll screw my pipes, and play a spring;
　And thus the weary night will end,
Till the tender kid and lamb-time bring
　Our pleasant simmer back again.

Syne, when the trees are in their bloom,
　And gowans glent o'er ilka fiel',
I'll meet my lass amang the broom,
　And lead ye to my simmer shiel',
Then far frae a' their scornfu' din,
　That mak' the kindly heart their sport,
We'll laugh, and kiss, and dance, and sing,
　And gar the langest day seem short.

An old song; from Herd's Collection.

CL.

BESSY BELL AND MARY GRAY.

Allan Ramsay.

O, Bessy Bell, and Mary Gray,
　They were twa bonnie lasses;
They biggit a bouir on yon burn-brae,
　And theekit it ower wi' rashes.
Fair Bessy Bell I lo'ed yestreen,
　And thocht I ne'er could alter;
But Mary Gray's twa pawky een
　They gar my fancy falter.

Bessy's hair's like a lint-tap,
  She smiles like a May morning,
When Phœbus starts frae Thetis' lap,
  The hills with rays adorning:
White is her neck, saft is her hand,
  Her waist and feet fu' genty;
With ilka grace she can command:
  Her lips, O, wow! they're dainty.

But Mary's locks are like the craw,
  Her een like diamond's glances;
She's aye sae clean, redd-up, and braw;
  She kills whene'er she dances;
Blythe as a kid, wi' wit at will,
  She blooming, tight, and tall is;
And guides her airs sae gracefu' still:
  O, Jove, she's like thy Pallas.

Dear Bessie Bell and Mary Gray,
  Ye unco sair oppress us;
Our fancies jee between ye twa,
  Ye are sic bonnie lasses.
Wae's me! for baith I canna get;
  To ane by law we're stented;
Then I'll draw cuts, and tak' my fate,
  And be wi' ane contented.

CLI.

THE HIGHLAND LADDIE.

Allan Ramsay.

The Lawland lads think they are fine,
  But, O, they're vain and idly gawdy!

How much unlike the gracefu' mien,
  And manly looks of my Highland laddie.

   O my bonny Highland laddie,
   My handsome, charming Highland laddie;
   May heaven still guard and love reward,
   Our Lawland lass, and her Highland laddie.

If I were free at will to choose,
  To be the wealthiest Lawland lady,
I'd tak' young Donald without trews,
  With bonnet blue, and belted plaidie.

The brawest beau in burrows-town,
  In a' his airs, wi' art, made ready,
Compared to him, he's but a clown,
  He's finer far in 's tartan plaidie.

O'er benty hill wi' him I'll run,
  And leave my Lawland kin and daddie;
Frae winter's cauld and summer's sun,
  He'll screen me wi' his Highland plaidie.

A painted room, and silken bed,
  May please a Lawland laird and lady;
But I can kiss and be as glad,
  Behind a bush in 's Highland plaidie.

Few compliments between us pass;
  I ca' him my dear Highland laddie,
And he ca's me his Lawland lass,
  Syne rows me in beneath his plaidie.

Nae greater joy I'll e'er pretend,
  Than that his love prove true and steady,
Like mine to him, which ne'er shall end,
  While heaven preserves my Highland laddie.

The tune to which these words are sung is very old, it
was printed in 1687; but the old words are now lost.

CLII.

KIND ROBIN LO'ES ME.

Robin is my only jo,
Robin has the art to lo'e,
So to his suit I mean to bow,
  Because I ken he lo'es me.
Happy, happy was the shower,
That led me to his birken bower,
Whare first of love I felt the power,
  And ken'd that Robin lo'ed me.

They speak of napkins, speak of rings,
Speak of gloves and kissing strings,
And name a thousand bonnie things,
  And ca' them signs he lo'es me.
But I prefer a smack of Rob,
Sporting on the velvet fog,
To gifts as lang's a plaiden wob,
  Because I ken he lo'es me.

He's tall and sonsy, frank and free,
Lo'ed by a', and dear to me,
Wi' him I'd live, wi' him I'd die,
  Because my Robin lo'es me.

My titty Mary said to me,
Our courtship but a joke wad be,
And I, or lang, be made to see,
    That Robin didna lo'e me.

But little kens she what has been,
Me and my honest Rob between,
And in his wooing, O, sae keen,
    Kind Robin is that lo'es me.
Then fly, ye lazy hours, away,
And hasten on the happy day,
When "join your hands," Mess John shall say,
    And mak' him mine that lo'es me.

Till then let every chance unite,
To weigh our love, and fix delight,
And I'll look down on such wi' spite,
    Who doubt that Robin lo'es me.
O hey, Robin, quo' she,
O hey, Robin, quo' she,
O hey, Robin, quo' she,
    Kind Robin lo'es me.

From *Herd's Collection.* There are much older words
to the tune, but they would be unsuitable here.

CLIII.

I LO'E NE'ER A LADDIE BUT ANE.

I lo'e ne'er a laddie but ane ;
    He lo'es ne'er a lassie but me ;
He's willing to mak' me his ain ;
    And his ain I am willing to be.

He coft me a rockley o' blue,
  And a pair o' mittens o' green ;
The price was a kiss o' my mou' ;
  An' I paid him the debt yestreen.

CLIV.

LOCH-EROCH SIDE.

James Tytler.—Born 1747 ; Died 1805.

As I came by Loch-Eroch side,
  The lofty hills surveying,
The water clear, the heather blooms
  Their fragrance sweet conveying,
I met, unsought, my lovely maid,
  I found her like May morning ;
With graces sweet, and charms so rare,
  Her person all adorning.

How kind her looks, how blest was I,
  While in my arms I prest her !
And she her wishes scarce conceal'd,
  As fondly I caress'd her.
She said, If that your heart be true,
  If constantly you'll love me,
I heed not care, nor fortune's frowns,
  For nought but death shall move me.

But faithful, loving, true, and kind,
  For ever thou shalt find me ;
And of our meeting here so sweet,
  Loch-Eroch side shall mind me.

Enraptured then, " My lovely lass,"
　　I cried, " No more we'll tarry !
We'll leave the fair Loch-Eroch side,
　　For lovers soon should marry."

The author of this song was an 'obscure tippling but extraordinary body commonly called Balloon Tytler, from his having projected a balloon : a mortal who, though he drudges about Edinburgh as a common printer, with leaky shoes, a sky-lighted hat, and knee-buckles as unlike as George-by-the-grace-of-God and Solomon-the-son-of-David, yet that same unknown drunken mortal is author and compiler of three-fourths of Elliot's pompous *Encyclopædia Britannica,* which he composed at half-a-guinea a week !'—*Burns.*

CLV.

THE YOUNG LAIRD AND EDIN-BURGH KATIE.

Allan Ramsay.

Now wat ye wha I met yestreen,
　　Coming down the street, my jo?
My mistress, in her tartan screen,
　　Fu' bonnie, braw, and sweet, my jo.
My dear, quoth I, thanks to the nicht
　　That never wiss'd a lover ill,
Sin' ye're out o' your mither's sicht,
　　Let's tak' a walk up to the hill.

Oh, Katie, wilt thou gang wi' me,
　　And leave the dinsome toun a while?
The blossom's sprouting frae the tree,
　　And a' the simmer's gaun to smile.

The mavis, nightingale, and lark,
  The bleating lambs and whistling hynd,
In ilka dale, green shaw, and park,
  Will nourish health, and glad your mind.

Sune as the clear gudeman o' day
  Bends his morning draught o' dew,
We'll gae to some burn-side and play,
  And gather flouirs to busk your brow.
We'll pou the daisies on the green,
  The lucken-gowans frae the bog;
Between hands, now and then, we'll lean
  And sport upon the velvet fog.

There's, up into a pleasant glen,
  A wee piece frae my father's tower,
A canny, saft, and flowery den,
  Which circling birks have made a bower.
Whene'er the sun grows high and warm,
  We'll to the caller shade remove;
There will I lock thee in my arm,
  And love and kiss, and kiss and love.

The first stanza belongs to an older song.

CLVI.

MUIRLAND WILLIE.

Hearken, and I will tell ye how,
Young Muirland Willie came to woo;
'Tho' he could neither say nor do,
  The truth I tell to you.
But aye, he cries, whate'er betide,
Maggie I'se ha'e to be my bride.

On his gray yade as he did ride,
Wi' durk and pistol by his side,
He prick'd her on wi' meikle pride,
    Wi' meikle mirth and glee,
Out o'er yon moss, out o'er yon muir
Till he came to her daddy's door.

Goodman, quoth he, be ye within,
I'm come your dochter's love to win,
I carena for making meikle din,
    What answer gi'e ye me?
Now wooer, quoth he, wou'd you light down,
I'll gi'e ye my dochter's love to win.

Now, wooer, sin' ye are lighted down,
Where do ye won, or in what town?
I think my dochter winna gloom,
    On sic a lad as you.
The wooer he stepp'd up the house,
And wow but he was wond'rous crouse.

I have three owsen in a pleugh,
Twa good gaun yads, and gear enough,
The place they ca' it Cadeneugh;
    I scorn to tell a lie:
Besides, I ha'e frae the great laird,
A peat-pat, and a lang kail yard.

The maid put on her kirtle brown,
She was the brawest in a' the town;
I wat on him she didna gloom,
    But blinkit bonnilie,
The lover he stended up in haste,
And gript her hard about the waist.

To win your love, maid, I'm come here,
I'm young and ha'e enough o' gear;
And for mysel' ye needna fear,
    Trowth try me whan ye like.
He took aff his bonnet, and spat in his chow,
He dightit his gab, and he prie'd her mou'.

The maiden blush'd and bing'd fu' law,
She hadna will to say him na,
But to her daddy she left it a',
    As they twa cou'd agree.
The lover he gied her the tither kiss,
Syne ran to her daddy, and tell'd him this.

Your dochter wadna say me na,
But to yoursel' she's left it a',
As we cou'd agree between us twa :
    Say, what ye'll gi'e me wi' her?
Now wooer, quoth he, I ha'e na meikle,
But sic's I ha'e ye's get a pickle.

A kilnfu' of corn I'll gi'e to thee,
Three soums o' sheep, twa good milk kye,
Ye's ha'e the wadding-dinner free ;
    Trowth I dow do nae mair.
Content, quoth he, a bargain be't,
I'm far frae hame, make haste, let's do't.

The bridal day it came to pass,
Wi' mony a blythsome lad and lass ;
But sicken a day there never was,
    Sic mirth was never seen.
This winsome couple strakit hands,
Mess John ty'd up the marriage bands.

And our bride's maidens were na few,
Wi' tap-knots, lug-knots, a' in blue,
Frae tap to tae they were braw new,
    And blinkit bonnilie.
Their toys and mutches were sae clean,
They glancèd in our lads's een.

Sic hirdum, dirdum, and sic din,
Wi' he o'er her, and she o'er him;
The minstrels they did never blin,
    Wi' meikle mirth and glee.
And aye they reel'd and aye they set,
And lads's lips with lasses' met.

'This lightsome ballad gives a particular drawing of those ruthless times, *whan thieves were rife*, and the lads went a wooing in their warlike habiliments, not knowing whether they would tilt with lips or launces'.—*Burns.*
It was first printed by Ramsay, as an old song.

CLVII.

WOO'D AND MARRIED AND A'.

The bride cam' out o' the byre,
    And, O, as she dighted her cheeks!
Sirs, I'm to be married the night,
    And has neither blankets nor sheets;
Has neither blankets nor sheets,
    Nor scarce a coverlet too;
The bride that has a' thing to borrow,
    Has e'en right muckle ado.

    Woo'd and married and a',
        Married and woo'd and a'!

And was she no very weel off,
  That was woo'd, and married and a'?

Out spake the bride's father,
  As he cam' in frae the pleugh,
O haud your tongue, my dochter,
  And ye'se get gear eneugh;
The stirk stands i' th' tether,
  And our braw bawsint yade,
Will carry ye hame your corn;
  What wad ye be at, ye jade?

Out spake the bride's mither,
  What deil needs a' this pride?
I had na a plack in my pouch
  That nicht I was a bride;
My gown was linsy-woolsy,
  And neer a sark ava;
And ye ha'e ribbons and buskins,
  Mae than ane or twa.

Out spake the bride's brither,
  As he came in wi' the kye:
Poor Willie wad ne'er ha'e ta'en ye,
  Had he kent ye as well as I;
For ye're baith proud and saucy,
  And no for a poor man's wife;
Gin I canna get a better,
  I'se never tak' ane i' my life.

Out spake the bride's sister,
  As she came in frae the byre;
O gin I were but married,
  It's a' that I desire;

But we poor folk maun live single,
　And do the best we can ;
I dinna care what I should want
　If I could but get a man.

Printed first in 1776 ; but it is of much older date.

CLVIII.

THE CARLE HE CAME O'ER THE CRAFT.

The carle he came o'er the craft,
　Wi' his beard new-shaven ;
He look'd at me as he'd been daft,—
　The carle trow'd that I wad ha'e him.
Hout awa' ! I winna ha'e him !
　Na, forsooth, I winna ha'e him !
For a' his beard new-shaven,
　Ne'er a bit o' me will ha'e him.

A siller brooch he ga'e me neist,
　To fasten on my curchie nookit ;
I wore 't a wee upon my breist,
　But soon, alake ! the tongue o't crookit ;
And sae may his ; I winna ha'e him !
　Na, forsooth, I winna ha'e him !
Twice-a-bairn's a lassie's jest ;
　Sae ony fool for me may ha'e him.

The carle has nae fault but ane ;
　For he has lands and dollars plenty,
But, waes me for him, skin and bane
　Is no for a plump lass o' twenty.

Hout awa', I winna ha'e him !
  Na, forsooth, I winna ha'e him !
What signifies his dirty riggs,
  And cash, without a man wi' them?

An old song, which Ramsay 'polished a little.' We
have omitted the last stanza.

CLIX.

BESS THE GAWKIE.

James Muirhead, D.D.—Born 1740 ; Died 1808.

Blythe young Bess to Jean did say,
Will ye gang to yon sunny brae,
Where flocks do feed, and herds do stray,
  And sport a while wi' Jamie?
Ah, na lass ! I'll no gang there,
Nor about Jamie tak' a care,
Nor about Jamie tak' a care,
  For he's ta'en up wi' Maggie.

For hark, and I will tell you, lass,
Did I not see young Jamie pass
Wi' meikle blytheness in his face,
  Out o'er the muir to Maggie.
I wat he ga'e her monie a kiss,
And Maggie took them ne'er amiss,
'Tween ilka smack pleased her wi' this,
  That Bess was but a gawkie :

For when a civil kiss I seek,
She turns her head and thraws her cheek,

And for an hour she'll hardly speak :
  Wha'd no ca' her a gawkie ?
But sure my Maggie has mair sense,
She'll gie a score without offence ;
Now gie me ane into the mense,
  And ye shall be my dawtie.

O Jamie, ye hae mony ta'en,
But I will never stand for ane
Or twa when we do meet again,
  So ne'er think me a gawkie.
Ah, na, lass, that canna be ;
Sic thoughts as thae are far frae me,
Or ony thy sweet face that see,
  E'er to think thee a gawkie.

But, whisht, nae mair o' this we'll speak,
For yonder Jamie does us meet :
Instead o' Meg he kiss'd sae sweet,
  I trow he likes the gawkie.
'O dear Bess, I hardly knew,
When I cam' by, your gown sae new ;
I think you've got it wet wi' dew.'
  Quoth she, 'That's like a gawkie ;

'It's wat wi' dew, and 'twill get rain,
And I'll get gowns when it is gane ;
Sae ye may gang the gate ye came,
  And tell it to your dawtie.'
The guilt appear'd on Jamie's cheek ;
He cried, 'O cruel maid, but sweet,
If I should gang anither gate,
  I ne'er could meet my dawtie.'

The lasses fast frae him they flew,
And left poor Jamie sair to rue
That ever Maggie's face he knew,
  Or yet ca'd Bess a gawkie.
As they gade ower the muir they sang,
The hills and dales wi' echo rang,
The hills and dales wi' echo rang,
  ' Gang o'er the muir to Maggie.'

" It is a beautiful song, and in the genuine Scot's taste,
we have few pastoral compositions, I mean the pastoral
of nature, that are equal to this."—*Burns.*

CLX.

DEAR ROGER, IF YOUR JENNY GECK.

Allan Ramsay.

Dear Roger, if your Jenny geck,
  And answer kindness with a slight,
Seem unconcern'd at her neglect,
  For women in our vows delight.
But them despise who are soon defeat,
  And with a simple face give way
To a repulse ; then be not blate,
  Push bauldly on and win the day.

When maidens, innocently young,
  Say aften what they never mean ;
Ne'er mind their pretty lying tongue,
  But tent the language o' their e'en ;

If these agree, and she persist
　　To answer all your love with hate,
Seek elsewhere to be better blest,
　　And let her sigh, when tis' too late.

CLXI.

THE CAULDRIFE WOOER.

There cam' a young man to my daddie's door,
My daddie's door, my daddie's door ;
There cam' a young man to my daddie's door,
　　Cam' seeking me to woo.

　　　And wow ! but he was a braw young lad,
　　　A brisk young lad, and a braw young lad,
　　　And wow ! but he was a braw young lad,
　　　　　Cam' seeking me to woo.

But I was baking when he came,
When he came, when he came ;
I took him in and gied him a scone,
　　To thowe his frozen mou'.

I set him in aside the bink ;
I ga'e him bread and ale to drink ;
But ne'er a blythe styme wad he blink,
　　Until his wame was fu'.

Gae, get ye gone, ye cauldrife wooer,
Ye sour-looking, cauldrife wooer !
I straightway show'd him to the door,
　　Saying, Come nae mair to woo.

There lay a deuk-dub before the door,
Before the door, before the door;
There lay a deuk-dub before the door,
    And there fell he, I trow!

Out cam' the gudeman, and high he shouted;
Out cam' the gudewife, and laigh she louted;
And a' the toun-neebors were gather'd about it;
    And there lay he, I trow!

Then out cam' I, and sneer'd and smil'd;
Ye cam' to woo, but ye're a' beguiled;
Ye've fa'en i' the dirt, and ye're a' befyled;
    We'll ha'e na' mair o' you!

From Herd's Collection.

CLXII.

I HA'E LAID A HERRING IN SAUT.

James Tytler.

I ha'e laid a herring in saut,
Lass gin ye lo'e me tell me now!
I ha'e brew'd a forpet o' maut,
An' I canna come ilka day to woo.
I ha'e a calf will soon be a cow,
Lass gin ye lo'e me tell me now!
I ha'e a pig will soon be a sow,
An' I canna come ilka day to woo.

I've a house on yonder muir,
Lass gin ye lo'e me tell me now!

Three sparrows may dance upon the floor,
An' I canna come ilka day to woo.
I ha'e a but an' I ha'e a ben,
Lass gin ye lo'e me tell me now !
I ha'e three chickens an' a fat hen,
An' I canna come ony mair to woo.

I've a hen wi' a happity leg,
Lass gin ye lo'e me tak' me now !
Which ilka day lays me an egg,
An' I canna come ilka day to woo.
I ha'e a kebbuck upon my shelf,
Lass gin ye lo'e me tak' me now ;
I downa eat it a' myself;
An' I winna come ony mair to woo.

CLXIII.

GREEN GROW THE RASHES, O.

R. Burns.

Green grow the rashes, O !
   Green grow the rashes, O !
The sweetest hours that e'er I spend,
   Are spent amang the lasses, O !

There's nought but care on ev'ry han'
   In ev'ry hour that passes, O ;
What signifies the life o' man,
   An' 'twere na for the lasses, O.

The warly race may riches chase,
   An' riches still may fly them, O ;

An' though at last they catch them fast,
   Their hearts can ne'er enjoy them, O.

But gie me a canny hour at e'en,
   My arms about my dearie, O ;
An' warly cares, an' warly men,
   May a' gae tapsalteerie, O.

For you so douce, ye sneer at this,
   Your nought but senseless asses, O ;
The wisest man the world e'er saw,
   He dearly lo'ed the lasses, O.

Auld Nature swears, the lovely dears,
   Her noblest work she classes, O ;
Her 'prentice han' she tried on man,
   And then she made the lasses, O.

CLXIV.

MAGGIE LAUDER.

Attributed to Francis Semple of Beltrees.
Circa 1650.

Wha wadna be in love
   Wi' bonnie Maggie Lauder?
A piper met her gaun to Fife,
   And speir'd what was't they ca'd her ;—
Right scornfully she answer'd him,
   Begone you hallanshaker !
Jog on your gate, you bletherskate,
   My name is Maggie Lauder.

Maggie, quo' he, now by my bags,
    I'm fidgin' fain to see thee;
Sit down by me, my bonnie bird,
    In troth I winna steer thee;
For I'm a piper to my trade,
    My name is Rab the Ranter;
The lasses loup as they were daft,
    When I blaw up my chanter.

Piper, quo' Meg, ha'e ye your bags,
    Or is your drone in order!
If ye be Rab, I've heard of you,
    Live ye upo' the border?
The lasses a', baith far and near,
    Have heard o' Rab the Ranter;
I'll shake my foot wi' right gude will,
    Gif you'll blaw up your chanter.

Then to his bags he flew wi' speed,
    About the drone he twisted;
Meg up and wallop'd o'er the green,
    For brawly could she frisk it.
Well done! quo' he—play up! quo' she;
    Well bobb'd! quo' Rab the Ranter;
'Tis worth my while to play indeed,
    When I ha'e sic a dancer.

Weel ha'e ye play'd your part, quo' Meg,
    Your cheeks are like the crimson;
There's nane in Scotland plays sae weel,
    Since we lost Habbie Simpson. *

* A celebrated Piper in Renfrewshire.

I've lived in Fife, baith maid and wife,
   These ten years, and a quarter;
Gin' ye should come to Anster fair,
   Speir ye for Maggie Lauder.

. CLXV.

FEE HIM, FATHER.

Saw ye Johnny comin', quo' she,
   Saw ye Johnny comin',
Saw ye Johnny comin', quo' she,
   Saw ye Johnny comin';
Saw ye Johnny comin', quo' she,
   Saw ye Johnny comin';
Wi' his blue bonnet on his head,
   An' his doggie rinnin', quo' she,
   An' his doggie rinnin'?

Fee him, father, fee him, quo' she,
   Fee him, father, fee him;
Fee him, father, fee him, quo' she,
   Fee him, father, fee him,
For he is a gallant lad,
   And a weel-doin';
And a' the wark about the house,
   Gaes wi' me when I see him, quo' she,
   Wi' me when I see him.

What will I do wi' him, hussy,
   What will I do wi' him?
He's ne'er a sark upon his back,
   And I ha'e nane to ga'e him.

I ha'e twa sarks into my kist,
  And ane o' them I'll gi'e him;
And for a merk o' mair fee
  Dinna stand wi' him, quo' she,
  Dinna stand wi' him.

For weel do I lo'e him, quo' she,
  Weel do I lo'e him;
For weel do I lo'e him, quo' she,
  Weel do I lo'e him.
O fee him, father, fee him, quo' she,
  Fee him, father, fee him;
He'll haud the pleugh, thrash in the barn,
  And crack wi' me at e'en, quo' she,
  And crack wi' me at e'en.

"This song, for genuine humour in the verses and
lively originality in the air, is unparalleled. I take it
to be very old."—*Burns.*

CLXVI.

WHEN SHE CAM' BEN.

O when she cam' ben she bobbit fu' law,
O when she cam' ben she bobbit fu' law,
And when she cam' ben, she kiss'd Cockpen,
And syne denied she did it at a'.

And wasna Cockpen richt saucy witha',
And wasna Cockpen richt saucy witha',
In leaving the dochter of a lord,
And kissing a collier lassie an' a'?

O never look doun, my lassie, at a',
O never look doun, my lassie, at a',
Thy lips are as sweet, and thy figure complete,
As the finest dame in castle or ha'.

'Though thou has nae silk and holland sae sma',
'Though thou has nae silk and holland sae sma',
Thy coat and thy sark are thy ain handywark,
And Lady Jean was never sae braw.

This is an old song with a few alterations by Burns.

CLXVII.

THE LAIRD O' COCKPEN.

Lady Nairne.

The Laird o' Cockpen, he's proud an' he's great,
His mind is ta'en up wi' the things o' the state,
He wanted a wife his braw house to keep;
But favour wi' wooin' was fashious to seek.

Doun by the dyke-side a lady did dwell,
At his table-head he thought she'd look well;
M'Clish's ae daughter o' Claverse-ha' Lee.
A pennyless lass wi' a lang pedigree.

His wig was weel pouther'd, as guid as when
        new,
His waiscoat was white, his coat it was blue:
He put on a ring, a sword, and cock'd hat—
And wha could refuse the Laird wi' a' that?

He took the gray mare, and rade cannilie ;
And rapped at the yet o' Claverse-ha' Lee ;
"Gae tell Mrs. Jean to come speedily ben ;
She's wanted to speak wi' the Laird o' Cockpen."

Mistress Jean was makin' elder flower wine ;
"And what brings the Laird at sic' a like time?"
She put off her apron, and on her silk goun,
Her mutch wi' red ribbons, and gaed awa' doun.

And when she cam' ben, he boued fu' low ;
And what was his errand he soon let her know.
Amazed was the Laird when the Lady said, Na,
And wi' a laigh curtsie she turned awa'.

Dumfounder'd he was, but nae sigh did he gie ;
He mounted his mare and rade cannilie ;
And often he thought, as he gaed through the
    glen,
She's daft to refuse the Laird o' Cockpen.

And now that the Laird his exit had made,
Mistress Jean she reflected on what she had
    said ;
"Oh ! for ane I'll get better, it's waur I'll get
    ten—
I was daft to refuse the Laird o' Cockpen."

Neist time that the Laird and the lady were
    seen,
They were gaun arm and arm to the kirk on the
    green:

Now she sits in the ha' like a weel-tappit hen,
But as yet there's nae chickens appear'd at
    Cockpen.

Miss Ferrier, who wrote *Marriage*, *Destiny*, etc., added
the last two verses.

CLXVIII.

ROBIN TAMSON.

Alexander Rodger.—Born 1784; Died 1846.

My mither men't my auld breeks,
    An' wow! but they were duddy,
And sent me to get Mally shod
    At Robin Tamsons' smiddy;
The smiddy stands beside the burn
    That wimples through the clachan,
I never yet gae by the door,
    But aye I fa' a-laughin'.

For Robin was a wealthy carle,
    And had ae bonnie dochter,
Yet ne'er wad let her tak' a man,
    Though mony lads had sought her;
And what think ye o' my exploit?—
    The time our mare was shoeing,
I slippit up beside the lass,
    An' briskly fell a-wooing.

An' aye she e'ed my auld breeks,
    The time that we sat crackin',

Quo' I, my lass, ne'er mind the clouts,
　　I've new anes for the makin';
But gin ye'll just come hame wi' me,
　　An' lea' the carle, your father,
Ye'se get my breeks to keep in trim,
　　Mysel', an' a' thegither.

Deed, lad, quo' she, your offer's fair,
　　I really think I'll tak' it,
Sae, gang awa', get out the mare,
　　We'll baith slip on the back o't;
For gin I wait my father's time,
　　I'll wait till I be fifty;
But na;—I'll marry in my prime,
　　An' mak' a wife most thrifty.

Wow! Robin was an angry man,
　　At tyning o' his dochter;
Through a' the kintra-side he ran,
　　An' far an' near he sought her;
But when he cam' to our fire-end,
　　An' fand us baith thegither,
Quo' I, gudeman, I've ta'en your bairn,
　　An' ye may tak' my mither.

Auld Robin grin'd, an' sheuk his pow,
　　Guid sooth! quo' he, you're merry,
But I'll just tak' ye at your word,
　　An' end this hurry-burry;
So Robin an' our auld wife
　　Agreed to creep thegither;
Now I hae Robin Tamson's pet,
　　An' Robin has my mither.

CLXIX.

THE DUSTY MILLER.

Hey, the dusty Miller,
  And his dusty coat,
He will win a shilling,
  Or he spend a groat.

Dusty was the coat,
  Dusty was the colour,
Dusty was the kiss
  That I got frae the Miller.

CLXX.

THE MILLER.

Sir John Clerk, Bart.—Born 1680; Died 1775.

Merry may the maid be,
  That marries the miller,
For foul day and fair day
  He's aye bringing till her;
Has aye a penny in his purse
  For dinner and for supper;
And gin she please, a good fat cheese,
  And lumps of yellow butter.

When Jamie first did woo me,
  I speir'd what was his calling;
Fair maid, says he, O come and see,
  Ye're welcome to my dwalling:

Though I was shy, yet I cou'd spy
  The truth of what he told me,
And that his house was warm and couth,
  And room in it to hold me.

Behind the door a bag of meal,
  And in the kist was plenty
Of good hard cakes his mither bakes,
  And bannocks were na scanty;
A good fat sow, a sleeky cow
  Was standin' in the byre;
While lazy puss with mealy mou'
  Was playing at the fire.

Good signs are these, my mither says,
  And bids me tak' the miller;
For foul day and fair day
  He's aye bringing till her;
For meal and malt she does na want,
  Nor anything that's dainty;
And now and then a keckling hen
  To lay her eggs in plenty.

In winter when the wind and rain
  Blaws o'er the house and byre,
He sits beside a clean hearth stane
  Before a rousing fire,
With nut-brown ale he tells his tale,
  Which rows him o'er fu' nappy:
Who'd be a king—a petty thing,
  When a miller lives so happy?

CLXXI.

TAK' IT, MAN, TAK' IT.

David Webster.

When I was a miller in Fife,
  Losh ! I thought that the sound o' the happer
Said, Tak' hame a wee flow to your wife,
  To help to be brose to your supper.
Then my conscience was narrow and pure,
  But someway by random it rackit;
For I liftet twa neivefu' or mair,
  While the happer said, Tak' it, man, tak' it.

    Then hey for the mill and the kill,
      The garland and gear for my cogie,
    And hey for the whiskey and yill,
      That washes the dust frae my craigie.

Although it's been lang in repute,
  For rogues to make rich by deceiving :
Yet I see that it disna weel suit
  Honest men to begin to the thieving.
For my heart it gaed dunt upon dunt,
  Od, I thought ilka dunt it wad crackit ;
Sae I flang frae my neive what was in't,
  Still the happer said, Tak' it, man, tak' it.

A man that's been bred to the plough,
  Might be deav'd with its clamorous clapper ;
Yet there's few but would suffer the sough,
  After kenning what's said by the happer.

I whiles thought it scoff'd me to scorn,
　Saying, Shame, is your conscience no chackit;
But when I grew dry for a horn,
　It chang'd aye to 'Tak' it, man, tak' it.

The smugglers whiles cam wi' their packs,
　'Cause they kent that I liked a bicker,
Sae I bartered whiles wi' the gowks,
　Gi'ed them grain for a soup o' their liquor.
I ha'e lang been accustomed to drink,
　And aye when I purposed to quat it,
The thing wi' its clapertie clink,
　Said aye to me, 'Tak' it, man, tak' it.

But the warst thing I did in my life,
　Nae doubt but ye'll think I was wrang o't.
Od, I tauld a bit bodie in Fife
　A' my tale, and he made a bit sang o't.
I have aye had a voice a' my days,
　But for singin' I ne'er got the knack o't;
Yet I try whiles, just thinking to please
　My frien's here, wi' 'Tak' it, man, tak' it.

Printed 1835.

CLXXII.

A LASS WITH A LUMP OF LAND.

Allan Ramsay.

Gie me a lass with a lump of land,
　And we for life shall gang thegither,
Tho' daft or wise, I'll ne'er demand,
　Or black or white, it mak's na whether.

I'm aff with wit, and beauty will fade,
   And blood alane's no worth a shilling.
But she that's rich, her market's made,
   For ilka charm about her's killing.

Gi'e me a lass with a lump of land,
   And in my bosom I'll hug my treasure :
Gin I had ance her gear in my hand,
   Should love turn dowf, it will find pleasure.
Laugh on wha likes, but, there's my hand,
   I hate with poortith, tho' bonny, to meddle.
Unless they bring cash, or a lump of land,
   They'se never get me to dance to their fiddle.

There's meikle good love in bands and bags,
   And siller and gowd's a sweet complexion ;
But beauty and wit, and virtue in rags,
   Have tint the art of gaining affection :
Love tips his arrows with woods and parks,
   And castles, and rigs, and muirs and meadows,
And naething can catch our modern sparks,
   But well-tocher'd lasses, or jointured widows.

CLXXIII.

COME UNDER MY PLAIDIE.

Hector Macneil.—Born 1746; Died 1818.

Come under my plaidie; the night's gaun to fa';
Come in frae the cauld blast, the drift, and the
     snaw :
Come under my plaidie, and sit down beside me :
There's room in't, dear lassie, believe me, for twa.

P

Come under my plaidie, and sit down beside me ;
I'll hap ye frae every cauld blast that can blaw :
Come under my plaidie, and sit down beside me :
There's room in't, dear lassie, believe me, for twa.

Gae 'wa wi' your plaidie ! auld Donald, gae 'wa,
I fear na the cauld blast, the drift, nor the snaw !
Gae 'wa wi' your plaidie ! I'll no sit beside ye ;
Ye micht be my gutcher ! auld Donald, gae 'wa.
I'm gaun to meet Johnnie—he's young and he's
         bonnie ;
He's been at Meg's bridal, fu' trig and fu' braw !
Nane dances sae lichtly, sae gracefu', or tichtly,
His cheek's like the new rose, his brow's like the
         snaw !

Dear Marion, let that flee stick fast to the wa' :
Your Jock's but a gowk, and has naething ava ;
The haill o' his pack he has now on his back ;
He's thretty, and I am but three score and twa.
Be frank now and kindly—I'll busk ye aye finely ;
To kirk or to market there'll few gang sae braw ;
A bein house to bide in, a chaise for to ride in,
And flunkies to 'tend ye as aft as ye ca'.

My father aye tauld me, my mother and a',
Ye'd mak' a gude husband, and keep me aye
         braw ;
It's true I lo'e Johnnie ; he's young and he's
         bonnie :
But wae's me ! I ken he has naething ava !
I ha'e little tocher : ye've made a gude offer ;
I'm now mare than twenty, my time is but sma' !

Sae gi'e me your plaidie : I'll creep in beside ye ;
I thocht ye'd been aulder than three score and
    twa.

She crapt in ayont him, beside the stane wa',
Whare Johnnie was listnin' and heard her tell a' :
The day was appointed ! his proud heart it dunted,
And stack 'gainst his side, as if burstin' in twa.
He wandered hame wearie, the nicht it was
    drearie,
And, thowless, he tint his gate 'mang the deep
    snaw :
The howlet was screamin', while Johnnie cried,
    Women
Wad marry Auld Nick, if he'd keep them aye braw.

CLXXIV.

JAMIE O' THE GLEN.

Auld Rob, the laird o' muckle land,
  To woo me was na very blate,
But spite o' a' his gear he fand
  He cam' to woo a day ower late.

    A lad sae blythe, sae fu' o' glee,
      My heart did never ken,
    And nane can gi'e sic joy to me
      As Jamie o' the glen.

My minnie grat like daft, and rair'd,
  To gar me wi' her will comply,
But still I wadna hae the laird,
  Wi' a' his ousen, sheep, and kye.

Ah, what are silks and satins braw?
　What's a' his warldly gear to me?
They're daft that cast themsel's awa',
　Where nae content or love can be.

I cou'dna bide the silly clash
　Cam hourly frae the gawky laird !
And sae, to stop his gab and fash,
　Wi' Jamie to the kirk repair'd.

Now ilka summer's day, sae lang,
　And winter's, clad wi' frost and snaw,
A tunefu' lilt and bonnie sang
　Aye keep dull care and strife awa'.

Printed first in *Johnson's Musical Museum ;* but it is
of much older date.

CLXXV.

TWINE WEEL THE PLAIDEN.

O, I ha'e lost my silken snood,*
　That tied my hair sae yellow ;

* 'The *snood* or riband, with which a Scottish lass
braided her hair, had an emblematical signification, and
applied to her maiden character.　It was exchanged for
the *curch, toy,* or coif, when she passed, by marriage, into
the matron state.　But if the damsel was so unfortunate
as to lose pretensions to the name of maiden, without
gaining a right to that of matron, she was neither per-
mitted to use the snood, nor advanced to the graver
dignity of the curch.　In old Scottish songs there occur
many sly allusions to such misfortune, as in the old words
to the popular tune of "O'er the Muir amang the
heather."'—*Scott.*

I've gi'en my heart to the lad I lo'ed,
   He was a gallant fellow.

    And twine it weel, my bonnie dow,
      And twine it weel the plaiden ;
    The lassie lost her silken snood,
      In pu'ing o' the breckan.

He praised my een sae bonnie blue,
   Sae lily-white my skin, O,
And syne he prie'd my bonnie mou',
   And said it was nae sin, O.

But he has left the lass he lo'ed,
   His own true love forsaken ;
Which gars me sair to greet the snood,
   I lost amang the breckan.

This song can be traced no farther back than *Johnson's Musical Museum*, although it is understood to be much older.

CLXXVI.

SOMEBODY.

R. Burns.

My heart is sair—I daurna tell—
   My heart is sair for somebody ;
I could wake a winter night,
   For the sake of somebody.

    Ochon, for somebody !
    Och hey, for somebody !

I could range the warld round,
　For the sake of somebody.

Ye powers that smile on virtuous love,
　O, sweetly smile on somebody !
Frae ilka danger keep him free,
　And send me safe my somebody.

　　Ochon, for somebody !
　　Och hey, for somebody !
　I wad do—what wad I not?—
　　For the sake of somebody.

Burns has borrowed some of the lines of this song from one by Ramsay.

CLXXVII.

TIBBIE FOWLER.

Tibbie Fowler o' the Glen,
　There's ower mony wooin' at her ;
Tibbie Fowler o' the Glen,
　There's ower mony wooin' at her.

　　Wooin' at her, pu'in' at her,
　　　Courtin' her. and canna get her.
　　Filthy elf, it's for her pelf,
　　　That a' the lads are wooin' at her.

Ten cam' east, and ten cam' west ;
　Ten cam' rowin' ower the water ;
Twa cam' down the lang dyke-side ;
　There's twa-and-thirty wooin' at her.

There's seven but, and seven ben,
  Seven in the pantry wi' her;
Twenty head about the door:
  There's ane-and-forty wooin' at her!

She's got pendles in her lugs:
  Cockle-shells wad set her better!
High-heel'd shoon, and siller tags,
  And a' the lads are wooin' at her.

Be a lassie e'er sae black.
  An' she hae the name o' siller,
Set her up on Tintock-tap,
  The wind will blaw a man till her.

Be a lassie e'er sae fair,
  An' she want the penny siller,
A flie may fell her in the air,
  Before a man be even'd till her.

The first complete copy of these words was printed in *Johnson's Musical Museum.*

CLXXVIII.

WHEN MAGGY GANGS AWAY.

James Hogg.

O, what will a' the lads do
  When Maggy gangs away?
O, what will a' the lads do
  When Maggy gangs away?

There's no a heart in a' the glen
  That disna dread the day.
O, what will a' the lads do
  When Maggy gangs away?

Young Jock has ta'en the hill for't—
  A waefu' wight is he;
Poor Harry's ta'en the bed for't,
  An' laid him doun to dee;
An' Sandy's gane unto the kirk,
  An's learning fast to pray.
And, O, what will the lads do
  When Maggy gangs away?

The young laird o' the Lang Shaw
  Has drunk her health in wine;
The priest has said—in confidence—
  The lassie was divine:
And that is mair in maiden's praise
  Than ony priest should say:
But, O, what will the lads do
  When Maggy gangs away?

The wailing in our green glen
  That day will quaver high;
'Twill draw the red-breast frae the wood,
  The laverock frae the sky;
The fairies frae their beds o' dew
  Will rise and join the lay:
An' hey! what a day 'twill be
  When Maggy gangs away!

CLXXIX.

COMIN' THRO' THE RYE.

Coming through the rye, poor body,
  Coming through the rye,
She draiglet a' her petticoatie,
  Coming through the rye.

    Oh Jenny's a' wat poor body,
     Jenny's seldom dry :
    She draiglet a' her petticoatie,
     Coming through the rye.

Gin a body meet a body—
  Coming through the rye,
Gin a body kiss a body—
  Need a body cry?

Gin a body meet a body
  Coming through the glen,
Gin a body kiss a body—
  Need the warld ken?

There are many versions of this old song. We give the
one which Burns chose for *Johnson's Musical Museum.*

CLXXX.

THE WAYWARD WIFE.

Janet Graham.—Born 1724; Died 1805.

Alas ! my son, you little know
The sorrows that from wedlock flow,
Farewell to every day of ease,
When you have got a wife to please.

Sae bide you yet, and bide you yet
Ye little ken what's to betide you yet,
The half of that will gane you yet,
If a wayward wife obtain you yet.

Sometimes the rock, sometimes the reel,
Or some piece of the spinning-wheel
She'll drive at you, my bonnie chiel ;
And then she'll send you to the deil.

When I like you was young and free.
I valued not the proudest she ;
Like you I vainly boasted then,
That men alone were born to reign.

Great Hercules and Samson too,
Were stronger men than I or you,
Yet they were baffled by their dears,
And felt the distaff and the shears.

Stout gates of brass and well-built walls,
Are proof 'gainst swords and cannon balls
But nought is found by sea or land.
That can a wayward wife withstand.

CLXXXI.

THE AULD GOODMAN. *

Late in an evening forth I went,
    A little before the sun gaed down ;
And then I chanced by accident,
    To light on a battle new begun.

Auld Goodman means here, *late Husband.*

A man and his wife were faun in a strife;
  I canna weel tell how it began
But aye she wail'd her wretched life,
  And cried ever, Alake, my auld goodman !

The auld goodman that thou tells of,
  The country kens where he was born,
Was but a puir silly vagabond.
  And ilka ane leuch him to scorn :
For he did spend and mak' an end
  Of gear that his forefathers wan ;
He gart the poor stand frae the door :
  Sae tell nae mair of thy auld goodman.

My heart. alake, is like to break.
  When I think on my winsome John ;
His blinking e'e, and gait sae free,
  Was naething like thee, thou dozent drone.
His rosy face and flaxen hair,
  And skin as white as ony swan,
Was large and tall, and comely withal ;
  And thou'lt never be like my auld goodman.

Why dost thou pleen? I thee mainteen ;
  For meal and maut thou disna want :
But thy wild bees I canna please,
  Now when our gear 'gins to grow scant.
Of household stuff thou hast enough :
  Thou wants for neither pot nor pan ;
Of siclike ware he left thee bare :
  Sae tell nae mair of thy auld goodman.

This song is at least as old as the seventeenth century.

CLXXXII.

OUR GUDEMAN CAM' HAME AT E'EN.

Our gudeman cam' hame at e'en,
　And hame cam' he ;
And there he saw a saddle-horse,
　Where nae horse should be.

Oh how cam' this horse here ?
　How can this be ?
How cam' this horse here,
　Without the leave o' me ?

A horse ! quo' she :
　Ay, a horse, quo' he.
Ye auld dotard carl,
　And blinder mat ye be,
It's but a bonnie milk-cow
　My minnie sent to me.

A milk-cow, quo' he :
　Ay, a milk-cow, quo' she.
Far hae I ridden,
　And muckle hae I seen,
But a saddle on a cow's back
　Saw I never nane.

Our gudeman cam' hame at e'en,
　And hame cam' he ;
He spied a pair of jackboots
　Where nae boots should be.

What's this now, gudewife?
  What's this I see?
How cam' these boots here
  Without the leave o' me?

   Boots ! quo' she :
   Ay, boots, quo' he.
Ye auld dotard carl,
  I'll mat ye see,
It's but a pair of water-stoups
  The cooper sent to me.

   Water-stoups ! quo' he :
   Ay, water-stoups, quo' she.
Far hae I ridden,
  And far hae I gane,
But siller spurs on water-stoups
  Saw I never nane,

Our gudeman cam' hame at e'en,
  And hame cam' he ;
And there he saw a siller sword,
  Where nae sword should be.

What's this now, gudewife?
  What's this I see?
O how cam' this sword here,
  Without the leave o' me?

   A sword ! quo' she :
   Ay, a sword, quo' he.
Ye auld dotard carl,
  I'll mat ye see,

It's but a parridge spurtle
  My minnie sent to me.

    A parridge spurtle ! quo' he :
      Ay, a parridge spurtle, quo' she.
Weel, far hae I ridden,
  And muckle hae I seen,
But siller-handed parridge spurtles
  Saw I never nane.

Our gudeman cam' hame at e'en,
  And hame cam' he ;
There he spied a powder'd wig,
  Where nae wig should be.

What's this now, gudewife?
  What's this I see?
How cam' this wig here,
  Without the leave o' me?

    A wig ! quo' she :
      Ay, a wig, quo' he.
Ye auld dotard carl,
  I'll mat ye see,
It's naething but a clockin-hen
  My minnie sent to me.

    A clockin-hen ! quo' he :
      Ay, a clockin-hen, quo' she.
Far hae I ridden,
  And muckle hae I seen,
But powder on a clockin-hen
  Saw I never nane.

SCOTTISH SONG.

Our gudeman cam' hame at e'en,
   And hame cam' he;
And there he saw a muckle-coat,
   Where nae coat should be.

O how cam' this coat here?
   How can this be?
How cam' this coat here,
   Without the leave o' me?

   A coat! quo' she:
   Ay, a coat, quo' he.
Ye auld blind dotard carl,
   Blind mat ye be,
It's but a pair a blankets
   My minnie sent to me.

   Blankets! quo' he:
   Ay, blankets, quo' she.
Far hae I ridden,
   And muckle hae I seen,
But buttons upon blankets
   Saw I never nane.

Ben gaed our gudeman,
   And ben ga'ed he;
And there he spied a sturdy man
   Where nae man should be.

How cam' this man here?
   How can this be?
How cam' this man here,
   Without the leave o' me?

A man ! quo' she :
　Ay, a man, quo' he.
Poor blind body,
　And blinder mat ye be,
It's a new milking maid
　My mither sent to me.

A maid ! quo' he :
　Ay, a maid, quo' she,
Far hae I ridden,
　And muckle hae I seen,
But lang-bearded maidens
　Saw I never nane.

This capital old song was first printed by Herd, in 1776.

CLXXXIII.

GET UP AND BAR THE DOOR.

It fell about the Martinmas time,
　And a gay time it was then,
When our gudewife got puddings to mak' :
　And she boiled them in the pan.

The wind sae cauld blew south frae north.
　And blew into the floor :
Quoth our gudeman to our gudewife,
　" Gae out and bar the door."

" My hand is in my hussy'fskap,
　Gudeman, as ye may see ;
An' it shouldna' be barr'd this hunder year,
　It's no be barr'd for me."

They made a paction 'tween them twa,
  They made it firm and sure,
That whae'er should speak the foremost word,
  Should rise and bar the door.

Then by there cam' twa gentlemen,
  At twelve o'clock at night,
And they could neither see house nor ha',
  Nor coal nor candle light.

Now, whether is this a rich man's house?
  Or whether is it a poor?
But never a word wad ane o' them speak,
  For the barrin' of the door.

And first they ate the white puddings,
  And then they ate the black ;
Tho' muckle thought our gudewife to hersel',
  Yet ne'er a word she spak'.

Then said the ane unto the ither,
  " Here, man, tak' ye my knife ;
Do ye tak' aff the auld man's beard,
  And I'll kiss the gudewife."

" But there's nae water in the house,
  And what shall we do than?
What ails ye at the pudding-bree,
  That boils into the pan?"

Up then started our gudeman,
  An angry man was he ;
" Will ye kiss my wife before my e'en,
  And scad me wi' the pudding bree?"

Then up and started our gudewife,
  Gied three skips on the floor ;
"Goodman, ye've spak the foremost word,
  Get up and bar the door.

There is a translation of this song by Goethe, in which,
however, the *catastrophe* is somewhat different ; we have
been told that the version from which he translated had
been altered, unknown to him, by some foolish English
lady.

CLXXXIV.

HAP AND ROW.

William Creech.—Born 1745 ; Died 1815.

We'll hap and row, we'll hap and row,
  We'll hap and row the feetie o't ;
It is a wee bit weary thing.
  I downa bide the greetie o't.

And we pat on the wee bit pan,
  To boil the lick o' meatie o't ;
A cinder fell and spoil'd the plan,
  And burnt a' the feetie o't.

Fu' sair it grat, the puir wee brat,
  And aye it kick'd the feetie o't,
Till, puir wee elf, it tired itself ;
  And then began the sleepie o't.

The skirling brat nae parritch gat,
  When it gaed to the sleepie o't ;
It's waesome true, instead o' 'ts mou',
  They're round about the feetie o't.

CLXXXV.

ROBIN RED-BREAST.

Gude day now, bonny Robin,
  How lang ha'e ye been here?
I've been a bird about this bush
  This mair than twenty year.

But now I am the sickest bird
  That ever sat on brier;
And I wad mak' my testament,
  Gudeman, if ye wad hear.

Gar tak' this bonny neb o' mine,
  That picks upon the corn;
And gi'e't to the Duke of Hamilton,
  To be a hunting-horn.

Gar tak' thae bonnie feathers o' mine,
  The feathers o' my neb;
And gi'e to the Lady Hamilton,
  To fill a feather-bed.

Gar tak' this gude richt-leg o' mine,
  And mend the brig o' Tay;
It will be a post and pillar gude,
  It will neither bow nor gae.

And tak' this other leg o' mine,
  And mend the brig o' Weir;
It will be a post and pillar gude,
  It'll neither bow nor steer.

Gar tak' they bonnie feathers o' mine,
  The feathers o' my tail;
And gi'e to the lads o' Hamilton
  To be a barn flail.

And tak' thae bonnie feathers o' mine,
  The feathers o' my breast;
And gi'e them to the bonnie lad,
  Will bring to me a priest.

Now in there cam' my Lady Wren,
  Wi' mony a sigh and groan,
O what care I for a' the lads,
  If my wee lad be gone!

Then Robin turn'd him round about,
  E'en like a little king;
Gae pack ye out at my chamber-door,
  Ye little cutty-quean.

From Herd's collection, 1776.

CLXXXVI.

WILLIE WASTLE.

R. Burns.

Willie Wastle dwelt on Tweed,
  The spot they ca'd it Linkumdoddie;
Willie was a wabster gude,
  Cou'd stown a clue wi' ony bodie;
He had a wife was dour and din,
  O Tinkler Madgie was her mither:
    Sic a wife as Willie had,
      I wad nae gie a button for her.

She has an ee, she has but ane,
  The cat has twa the very colour;
Five rusty teeth, forbye a stump,
  A clapper tongue wad deave a miller;
A whiskin' beard about her mou',
  Her nose and chin they threaten ither:
    Sic a wife as Willie had,
    I wad na gie a button for her.

She's bow-hough'd, she's hein-shinn'd,
  Ae limpin' leg a hand-breed shorter;
She's twisted right, she's twisted left,
  To balance fair on ilka quarter:
She has a hump upon her breast,
  The twin o' that upon her shouther:
    Sic a wife as Willie had,
    I wad na gie a button for her.

Auld baudrans by the ingle sits,
  An' wi' her loof her face a washin';
But Willie's wife is nae sae trig,
  She dights her grunzie wi' a hushion:
Her walie nieves like midden-creels,
  Her face wad fyle the Logan-water:
    Sic a wife as Willie had.
    I wad na gie a button for her.

In Whitlocke * there is the following curious notice of a "William of the Wastle," cited by Carlyle,† which may, perhaps, have suggested the name in this song. In Feb., 1650, on Fenwick's demanding the surrender of

* *Memorials of English Affairs* (London, 1682), p. 464.
† *Cromwell's Letters and Speeches* (Library Edition), Vol. III., p. 116.

Hume Castle, its owner answered, 'That he knew not Cromwell, and for his castle, it was built upon a rock.' Four days afterwards, when the great guns were opened upon him, he sent another letter, as follows :—

> ' I, William of the Wastle,
> Am now in my castle ;
> And aw the dogs in the town
> Shanna gar me gang down.'

The mortars, however, were opened upon him, 'which did gar him gang down,' Carlyle says, 'more fool than he went up.'

CLXXXVII.

JANET MACBEAN.

Robert Nicoll.—Born 1814 ; Died 1837.

Janet Macbean a public keeps,
   An' a merry auld wife is she ;
An' she sells her yill wi' a jaunty air
   That wad please your heart to see.
Her drink's o' the best—she's hearty aye,
   An' her house is neat an' clean—
There's no an auld wife in the public line
   Can match wi' Janet Macbean.

She has aye a curtsey for the laird
   When he comes to drink his can,
An' a laugh for the farmer an' his wife,
   An' a joke for the farmer's man.
She toddles but an' she toddles ben,
   Like onie wee bit queen—
There's no an auld wife in the public line
   Can match wi' Janet Macbean.

The beggar wives gang a' to her,
   An' she sairs them wi' bread an' cheese:—
Her bread in bannocks an' cheese in whangs
   Wi' a blythe gudewill she gi'es.
Vow, the kintra-side will miss her sair
   When she's laid aneath the green—
There's no an auld wife in the public line
   Can match wi' Janet Macbean.

Amang alehouse wives she rules the roast;
   For upo' the Sabbath days
She puts on her weel hain'd tartan plaid
   An' the rest o' her Sabbath claes;
An' she sits, nae less ! in the minister's seat:
   Ilk psalm she lilts, I ween—
There's no an auld wife in the public line
   Can match wi' Janet Macbean.

CLXXXVIII.

WHISTLE, AND I'LL COME TO YOU, MY LAD.

R. Burns.

O, whistle, and I'll come to you, my lad ;
O, whistle, and I'll come to you, my lad ;
Tho' father, and mother, and a' should gae mad,
O, whistle, and I'll come to you, my lad.

But warily tent, when you come to court me,
And come na unless the back-yett be a-jee;
Syne up the back-stile, and let nae body see,
And come as ye were na comin' to me,
And come as ye were na comin' to me.

At kirk or at market, whene'er ye meet me,
Gang by me as though ye cared na a flie;
But steal me a blink o' your bonnie black e'e,
Yet look as ye were na lookin' at me,
Yet look as ye were na lookin' at me.

Aye vow and protest that ye care na for me,
And whyles ye may lichtly my beauty a wee;
But court na anither, though jokin' ye be,
For fear that she wyle your fancy frae me,
For fear that she wyle your fancy frae me.

Part IV.

CLXXXIX.

BRUCE'S ADDRESS.

R. Burns.

Scots, wha ha'e wi' Wallace bled;
Scots, wham Bruce has aften led !
Welcome to your gory bed,
   Or to victorie !
Now's the day, and now's the hour :
See the front of battle lour :
See approach proud Edward's pow'r—
   Chains and slaverie !

Wha will be a traitor knave?
Wha can fill a coward's grave?
Wha sae base as be a slave?
   Let him turn and flee !
Wha, for Scotland's king and law,
Freedom's sword will strongly draw.
Freeman stand, or freeman fa',
   Let him follow me !

By oppression's woes and pains,
By your sons in servile chains,
We will drain our dearest veins,
    But they shall be free.
Lay the proud usurpers low !
Tyrants fall in every foe !
Liberty's in every blow !
    Let us do or die !

' So long as there is warm blood in the heart of Scotch-
man or man, it will move in fierce thrills under this war-
ode ; the best, we believe, that ever was written by any
pen'.—*Carlyle.*

CXC.

CHARLIE IS MY DARLING.

Lady Nairne.

'Twas on a Monday morning,
    Richt early in the year,
That Charlie cam' to our toun,
    The young Chevalier.

    Oh, Charlie is my darling,
        My darling, my darling ;
    Charlie is my darling,
        The young Chevalier.

As he came marching up the street,
    The pipes played loud and clear ;
And a' the folk cam' running out
    To meet the Chevalier.

Wi' Hieland bonnets on their heads,
  And claymores bright and clear,
They've come to fight for Scotland's right,
  And the young Chevalier.

They've left their bonnie Hieland hills,
  Their wives and bairnies dear;
They've drawn the sword for Scotland's lord,
  And the young Chevalier.

CXCI.

KENMURE'S ON AND AWA'.

O, Kenmure's on and awa', Willie,
  O, Kenmure's on and awa';
And Kenmure's lord's the bravest lord
  That ever Galloway saw.

Success to Kenmure's band, Willie,
  Success to Kenmure's band!
There's no a heart that fears a Whig,
  That rides by Kenmure's hand.

Here's Kenmure's health in wine, Willie,
  Here's Kenmure's health in wine!
There ne'er was a coward o' Kenmure's blude,
  Nor yet o' Gordon's line.

O, Kenmure's lads are men, Willie,
  O, Kenmure's lads are men!
Their hearts and swords are metal true;
  And that their faes shall ken.

They'll live or die wi' fame, Willie,
   They'll live or die wi' fame ;
But sune wi' sound and victorie
   May Kenmure's lord come hame.

Here's Him that's far awa', Willie,
   Here's Him that's far awa';
And here's the flower that I lo'e best,
   The rose that's like the snaw.

In 1715, William Gordon, Viscount Kenmure, left Galloway with about 200 horsemen, and joined the Pretender at Preston in Lancashire. There he was made prisoner. He and many of his men were taken to London, where, with their arms pinioned, they were led on horseback through the chief streets, to their respective prisons, amidst the din of victorious music, and the yelling and hooting of the mob. Kenmure was beheaded on Tower Hill in 1716.

CXCII.

JOHNNIE COPE.

Adam Skirving.—Born 1719 ; Died 1803.

Cope sent a challenge frae Dunbar :—
Charlie, meet me an ye daur,
And I'll learn you the art o' war,
   If you'll meet wi' me i' the mornin.

   Hey, Johnnie Cope, are ye wauking yet ?
   Or are your drums a-beating yet ?
   If ye were wauking, I wad wait
      To gang to the coals i' the morning.

When Charlie look'd the letter upon,
He drew his sword the scabbard from :
Come follow me, my merry merry men,
  And we'll meet Johnnie Cope in the morning.

Now, Johnnie, be as good's your word,
Come let us try both fire and sword ;
And dinna flee away like a frighted bird,
  That's chased frae its nest in the morning.

When Johnnie Cope he heard of this,
He thought it wadna be amiss,
To ha'e a horse in readiness,
  To flee awa' in the morning.

Fy now, Johnnie, get up and rin,
The Highland bagpipes mak' a din ;
It is best to sleep in a hale skin,
  For 'twill be a bluidy morning.

When Johnnie Cope to Dunbar came,
They speer'd at him, Where's a' your men?
The deil confound me gin I ken,
  For I left them a' i' the morning.

Now, Johnnie, troth ye are na blate,
To come wi' the news o' your ain defeat,
And leave your men in sic a strait,
  Sae early in the morning.

Oh ! faith, quo' Johnnie, I got sic flegs
Wi' their claymores and philabegs ;

If I face them again, deil break my legs—
  So I wish you a' gude morning.

    Sir John Cope was tried by court-martial for his "foul flight" (as Colonel Gardiner called it) from the field at Prestonpans, 1715; but was acquitted.

CXCIII.

HE'S OWRE THE HILLS.

Lady Nairne.

He's owre the hills that I lo'e weel;
He's owre the hills we darena name,
He's owre the hills ayont Dumblane,
Wha soon will get his welcome hame.

My father's gane to fight for him,
My brithers winna bide at hame,
My mither greets and prays for them,
But deed she thinks they're no to blame.

The Whigs may scoff, the Whigs may jeer,
But ah! that love maun be sincere,
Which still keeps true whate'er betide,
And for his sake leaves a' beside.

His right these hills; his right these plains;
O'er Hieland hearts secure he reigns;
What lads e'er did our lads will do;
Were I a laddie, I'd follow him too.

Sae noble a look, sae princely an air,
Sae gallant and bold, sae young and sae fair;
Oh! did ye but see him, ye'd do as we've done;
Hear him but ance, to his standard you'll run.

CXCIV.

O WHERE, TELL ME WHERE.

Anne Macivar, afterwards Mrs. Grant.
Born 1755; Died 1838.

O where, tell me where, is your Highland laddie
    gone?
O where, tell me where, is your Highland laddie
    gone?
He's gone with streaming banners, where noble
    deeds are done,
And my sad heart will tremble till he come safely
    home.

O where, tell me where, did your Highland
    laddie stay?
O where, tell me where, did your Highland
    laddie stay?
He dwelt beneath the holly trees, beside the
    rapid Spey,
And many a blessing follow'd him, the day he
    went away.

O what, tell me what, does your Highland laddie
    wear?
O what, tell me what, does your Highland laddie
    wear?

A bonnet with a lofty plume, the gallant badge
　　of war,
And a plaid across the manly breast that yet
　　shall wear a star.

Suppose, ah suppose, that some cruel, cruel
　　wound
Should pierce your Highland laddie, and all
　　your hopes confound !
The pipe would play a cheering march, the
　　banners round him fly,
The spirit of a Highland chief would lighten in
　　his eye.

But I will hope to see him yet in Scotland's
　　bonnie bounds,
But I will hope to see him yet in Scotland's
　　bonnie bounds,
His native land of liberty shall nurse his glorious
　　wounds,
While wide through all our Highland hills his
　　warlike name resounds.

This song was written on the Marquis of Huntley's
departure for Holland, with the British forces, under the
command of Sir Ralph Abercromby, in 1799.

CXCV.

LEWIS GORDON.

Alexander Geddes, D.D.—Born 1737 ; Died 1802.

Oh ! send my Lewis Gordon hame
And the lad I daurna' name ;
Although his back be at the wa',
Here's to him that's far awa.

Hech hey ! my Highlandman !
My handsome, charming Highlandman !
Weel could I my true love ken,
Amang ten thousand Highlandmen.

Oh, to see his tartan trews,
Bonnet blue and laigh-heel'd shoes,
Philabeg aboon his knee !
That's the lad that I'll gang wi'.

This lovely lad of whom I sing,
Is fitted for to be a king ;
And on his breast he wears a star,
You'd take him for the god of war.

Oh, to see this princely one
Seated on his father's throne !
Our griefs would then a' disappear,
We'd celebrate the jub'lee year.

Lewis Gordon commanded a detachment for "the
Chevalier" in 1715. He died in France in 1754. ' It
needs not a Jacobite prejudice to be affected with this
song.'—*Burns.*

CXCVI.

CARLE, AN THE KING COME.

Carle, an the king come,
Carle, an the king come,
Thou shalt dance and I will sing,
Carle, an the king come.

An somebody were come again,
Then somebody maun cross the main ;
And every man shall ha'e his ain,
  Carle, an the king come.

I trow we swappit for the worse ;
We ga'e the boot and better horse ;
And that we'll tell them at the cross,
  Carle, an the king come.

    Cogie, an the king come,
    Cogie, an the king come,
    I'se be fou' and thou'se be toom,
      Cogie, an the king come.

CXCVII.

PEGGY, NOW THE KING'S COME.

Allan Ramsay.

    Peggy, now the king's come,
    Peggy, now the king's come,
    Thou may dance and I shall sing,
      Peggy, since the king's come.

Nae mair the hawkies shalt thou milk,
But change thy plaiding-coat for silk,
And be a lady of that ilk,
  Now, Peggy, since the king's come.

CXCVIII.

THE WHITE COCKADE.

My love was born in Aberdeen,
The bonniest lad that e'er was seen ;
But now he makes our hearts fu' sad—
He's ta'en the field wi' his white cockade.

O, he's a ranting, roving blade !
O, he's a brisk and a bonnie lad !
Betide what may, my heart is glad
To see my lad wi' his white cockade.

O, leeze me on the philabeg,
The hairy hough, and garter'd leg ;
But aye the thing that glads my e'e,
Is the white cockade aboon the bree.

I'll sell my rock, I'll sell my reel,
My rippling kame, and spinning wheel,
To buy my lad a tartan plaid,
A braidsword and a white cockade.

I'll sell my rokely and my tow,
My gude gray mare and hawket cow,
That ev'ry loyal Buchan lad
May tak' the field wi' his white cockade.

CXCIX.

O'ER THE WATER TO CHARLIE.

Come, boat me ower, come, row me ower,
Come, boat me ower to Charlie ;

I'll gi'e John Brown another half-crown,
  To boat me ower to Charlie.

        We'll o'er the water, and o'er the sea,
          We'll o'er the water to Charlie ;
        Come weel, come woe, we'll gather and go,
          And live or die wi' Charlie.

It's I lo'e weel my Charlie's name,
  Though some there be that abhor him ;
But O, to see Auld Nick gaun hame,
  And Charlie's faes before him !

I swear by moon and stars sae bricht,
  And the sun that glances early,
If I had twenty thousand lives,
  I'd die as aft for Charlie.

cc.

THE CAMPBELLS ARE COMING.

The Campbells are coming, O-ho, O-ho !
  The Campbells are coming, O-ho !
The Campbells are coming to bonnie Lochleven !
  The Campbells are coming, O-ho, O-ho !

Upon the Lomonds I lay, I lay ;
  Upon the Lomonds I lay ;
I lookit doun to bonnie Lochleven,
  And saw three perches play.

Great Argyle he goes before ;
  He makes the cannons and guns to roar ;

With sound of trumpet, pipe, and drum;
  The Campbells are coming, O-ho, O-ho!

The Campbells they are a' in arms,
  Their loyal faith and truth to show,
With banners rattling in the wind,
  The Campbells are coming O-ho, O-ho!

CCI.

THE WEE GERMAN LAIRDIE.

Wha the deil ha'e we gotten for a king,
  But a wee, wee German lairdie?
And, when we gaed to bring him hame,
  He was delving in his yairdie:
Sheughing kail, and laying leeks,
But the hose and but the breeks;
Up his beggar duds he cleeks—
  This wee, wee German lairdie.

And he's clapt down in our gudeman's chair,
  The wee, wee German lairdie;
And he's brought fouth o' foreign leeks,
  And dibbled them in his yairdie.
He's pu'd the rose o' English loons,
And broken the harp o' Irish clowns;
But our thistle taps will jag his thooms—
  This wee, wee German lairdie.

Come up amang our Highland hills,
  Thou wee, wee German lairdie,
And see the Stuart's lang-kail thrive
  We dibbled in our yairdie:

But if a stock ye dare to pu',
Or haud the yoking o' a plough,
We'll break your sceptre o'er your mou',
    Thou wee bit German lairdie.

Our hills are steep, our glens are deep,
    No fitting for a yairdie,
And our Norland thistles winna pu',
    Thou wee bit German lairdie :
And we've the trenching blades o' weir,
Wad lib ye o' your German gear—
We'll pass ye 'neath the claymore's shear,
    Thou feckless German lairdie !

Auld Scotland, thou'rt ower cauld a hole
    For nursin' siccan vermin ;
But the very dougs o' England's court
    They bark and howl in German !
Then keep thy dibble in thy ain hand,
    Thy spade but and thy yairdie,
For wha the deil ha'e we gotten for a king,
    But a wee, wee German lairdie ?

CCII.

WHA'LL BE KING BUT CHARLIE.

Lady Nairne.

The news frae Moidart cam' yestreen,
    Will soon gar mony ferlie,
For ships o' war have just come in,
    An' landed Royal Charlie.

Come thro' the heather, around him gather,
  Ye're a' the welcomer early ;
Around him cling wi' a' your kin ;
  For wha'll be king but Charlie ?

Come through the heather, around him gather,
  Come Ronald, come Donald, come a' thegither,
And crown him rightfu', lawful king ;
  For wha'll be king but Charlie ?

The Highland clans wi' sword in hand,
  Frae John o' Groats to Airlie,
Ha'e to a man declared to stand
  Or fa' wi' royal Charlie.

The Lowlands a', baith great an' sma',
  Wi' mony a lord an' laird, ha'e
Declared for Scotia's king an' law,
  An' spier ye wha but Charlie ?

There's ne'er a lass in a' the land,
  But vows baith late an' early,
To man she'll ne'er gi'e heart or hand,
  Wha wadna fecht for Charlie.

Then here's a health to Charlie's cause,
  An' be't complete and early,
His very name my heart's blood warms,—
  To arms for royal Charlie !

CCIII.

YE JACOBITES BY NAME.

R. Burns.

Ye Jacobites by name, give an ear, give an ear;
Ye Jacobites by name, give an ear;
Ye Jacobites by name,
Your fautes I will proclaim,
Your doctrines I maun blame—
You shall hear.

What is right, and what is wrang, by the law, by
the law?
What is right, and what is wrang, by the law?
What is right, and what is wrang?
A short sword, and a lang,
A weak arm, and a strang
For to draw.

What makes heroic strife, fam'd afar, fam'd afar?
What makes heroic strife, fam'd afar?
What makes heroic strife?
To whet th' assassin's knife,
Or hunt a parent's life
Wi' bluidie war.

Then let your schemes alone, in the state, in the
state;
Then let your schemes alone in the state;
Then let your schemes alone,
Adore the rising sun,
And leave a man undone
To his fate.

CCIV.

STRATHALLAN'S LAMENT.

R. Burns.

Thickest night, surround my dwelling !
   Howling tempests, o'er me rave !
Turbid torrents, wintry swelling,
   Roaring by my lonely cave.
Crystal streamlets, gently flowing,
   Busy haunts of base mankind,
Western breezes, softly blowing,
   Suit not my distracted mind.

In the cause of right engaged,
   Wrongs injurious to redress,
Honour's war we strongly waged,
   But the heavens denied success.
Ruin's wheel has driven o'er us,
   Not a hope that dare attend,
The wide world is all before us—
   But a world without a friend !

This song was written to describe the feelings of James
Drummond, Viscount of Strathallan, who, after his father's
death at Culloden, escaped, with several of his country-
men, to France, where he died in exile.

CCV.

ADIEU FOR EVERMORE.

It was a' for our rightfu' king,
   We left fair Scotland's strand !

It was a' for our richtfu' king,
  We e'er saw Irish land, my dear,
  We e'er saw Irish land.

Now a' is done that men can do,
  And a' is done in vain ;
My love, my native land, fareweel,
  For I maun cross the main, my dear,
  For I maun cross the main.

He turn'd him right and round about
  Upon the Scottish shore,
He gave his bridle-reins a shake,
  With, Adieu for evermore, my dear,
  · With, Adieu for evermore.

The sodger frae the war returns,
  The sailor frae the main ;
But I ha'e parted frae my love,
  Never to meet again, my dear,
  Never to meet again.

When day is gane, and nicht is come,
  And a' folk bound to sleep,
I think on him that's far awa',
  The lee-lang night, and weep, my dear,
  The lee-lang night, and weep.

This song refers to the insurrection in Ireland, under
James II., which ended in the Battle of the Boyne.

CCVI.

WAE'S ME FOR PRINCE CHARLIE.

William Glen.—Died 1826.

A wee bird cam' to our ha' door,
  He warbled sweet and clearly,
An' aye the o'ercome o' his sang
  Was 'Wae's me for Prince Charlie !'
Oh ! when I heard the bonnie bird,
  The tears cam' happin' rarely,
I took my bannet aff my head,
  For weel I lo'ed Prince Charlie.

Quoth I, 'My bird, my bonnie bonnie bird,
  Is that a sang ye borrow,
Are these some words ye've learnt by heart,
  Or a lilt o' dool an' sorrow ?'
'Oh ! no, no, no,' the wee bird sang,
  ' I've flown sin' mornin' early,
But sic a day o' wind and rain—
  Oh ! wae's me for Prince Charlie !

' On hills that are, by right, his ain
  He roves a lanely stranger,
On every side he's press'd by want,
  On every side is danger ;
Yestreen I met him in a glen,
  My heart maist bursted fairly,
For sadly chang'd indeed was he—
  Oh ! wae's me for Prince Charlie !

‘ Dark night cam’ on, the tempest roar’d
　　Loud o’er the hills an’ valleys ;
An’ whare was’t that your Prince lay down
　　Whase hame should be a palace ?
He row’d him in a Highland plaid,
　　Which cover’d him but sparely,
An’ slept beneath a bush o’ broom—
　　Oh ! wae’s me for Prince Charlie !’

But now the bird saw some red coats,
　　An’ he shook his wings wi’ anger,
‘ Oh ! this is no a land for me,
　　I’ll tarry here nae langer.’
He hover’d on the wing a while
　　Ere he departed fairly,
But weel I mind the fareweel strain
　　Was, ‘ Wae’s me for Prince Charlie !’

CCVII.

COLONEL GARDINER.

Sir Gilbert Elliot.

’Twas at the hour of dark midnight,
　　Before the first cock’s crowing,
When westland winds shook Stirling’s towers
　　With hollow murmurs blowing ;
When Fanny fair, all woe begone,
　　Sad on her bed was lying,
And from the ruin’d towers she heard
　　The boding screech-owl crying.

O dismal night ! she said, and wept,
  O night presaging sorrow,
O dismal night ! she said, and wept,
  But more I dread to-morrow.
For now the bloody hour draws nigh,
  Each host to Preston bending ;
At morn shall sons their fathers slay,
  With deadly hate contending.

Even in the visions of the night,
  I saw fell death wide sweeping ;
And all the matrons of the land,
  And all the virgins, weeping.
And now she heard the massy gates
  Harsh on their hinges turning ;
And now, through all the castle, heard
  The woeful voice of mourning.

Aghast, she started from her bed,
  The fatal tidings dreading ;
O speak, she cried, my father's slain !
  I see, I see him bleeding !
A pale corse on the sullen shore,
  At morn, fair maid, I left him ;
Even at the threshold of his gate,
  The foe of life bereft him.

Bold, in the battle's front he fell,
  With many a wound deformed ;
A braver knight, nor better man,
  This fair Isle ne'er adorned.
While thus he spoke the grief-struck maid
  A deadly swoon invaded ;

Lost was the lustre of her eyes,
   And all her beauty faded.

Sad was the sight, and sad the news,
   And sad was our complaining ;
But oh ! for thee, my native land,
   What woes are still remaining !
But why complain ? the hero's soul
   Is high in heaven shining :
May Providence defend our Isle
   From all our foes designing

Colonel Gardiner, the hero of this song, fell at Preston-
pans in 1745. It is distinguished by being one of the
very few which are extant, not on the Stuart side.

CCVIII.

MACPHERSON'S RANT.

I've spent my time in rioting,
   Debauch'd my health and strength ;
I've pillaged, plunder'd, murdered,
   But now, alas, at length,
I'm brought to punishment direct ;
   Pale death draws near to me ;
This end I never did project,
   To hang upon a tree.

To hang upon a tree, a tree !
   That curs'd unhappy death !
Like to a wolf to worried be,
   And choaked in the breath.

My very heart wad surely break
  When this I think upon,
Did not my courage singular
  Bid pensive thoughts begone.

No man on earth that draweth breath
  More courage had than I;
I dared my foes unto their face,
  And would not from them fly.
This grandeur stout I did keep out,
  Like Hector, manfullie;
Then wonder one like me so stout
  Should hang upon a tree.

The Egyptian band I did command,
  With courage more by far,
Than ever did a general
  His soldiers in the war.
Being fear'd by all, both great and small,
  I lived most joyfullie :
Oh, curse upon this fate of mine,
  To hang upon a tree !

As for my life, I do not care,
  If justice would take place,
And bring my fellow-plunderers
  Unto the same disgrace.
But Peter Brown, that notour loon,
  Escap'd, and was made free :
Oh, curse upon this fate of mine,
  To hang upon a tree !

Both law and justice buried are,
　　And fraud and guile succeed;
The guilty pass unpunished,
　　If money intercede.
The Laird of Grant, that Highland saunt,
　　His mighty majestie,
He pleads the cause of Peter Brown,
　　And lets Macpherson die.

The dest'ny of my life contrived
　　By those whom I obliged,
Rewarded me much ill for good,
　　And left me no refuge.
For Braco Duff, in rage enough,
　　He first laid hands on me;
And if that death did not prevent,
　　Avenged would I be.

As for my life, it is but short,
　　When I shall be no more;
To part with life I am content,
　　As any heretofore.
Therefore, good people all, take heed,
　　This warning take by me,
According to the lives you lead,
　　Rewarded you shall be.

　　Macpherson was a noted freebooter, executed at Banff in 1700. He is said to have played this "rant" at the gallows, and then offered his fiddle to any Macpherson who would consent to play it again over his dead body; none came forward, so he threw it on the ground and crashed it to pieces under his feet.

CCIX.

MACPHERSON'S FAREWELL.

R. Burns.

Farewell, ye dungeons dark and strong,
  The wretch's destinie !
Macpherson's time will not be long
  On yonder gallows tree.

    Sae rantingly, sae wantonly,
      Sae dauntingly gaed he,
      He play'd a spring, and danced it round,
      Below the gallows tree !

Oh, what is death, but parting breath?
  On mony a bluidy plain
I've daur'd his face, and in this place
  I scorn him yet again.

Untie these bands frae aff my hands,
  And bring to me my sword;
And there's no a man in all Scotland
  But I'll brave him at a word.

I've lived a life of sturt and strife;
  I die by treacherie :
It burns my heart I must depart,
  And not avenged be.

Now farewell, light, thou sunshine bright,
  And all beneath the sky !
May coward shame distain his name,
  The wretch that dares not die !

CCX.

ARMSTRONG'S GOOD-NIGHT.

O this is my departing time !
  For here nae langer maun I stay :
There's not a friend or foe of mine
  But wishes that I were away.

What I have done for lack o' wit,
  I never, never can recall ;
I hope you're a' my friends as yet :
  Good-night and joy be wi' you all.

'These verses are said to have been composed by one of the Armstrongs, executed for the murder of Sir John Carmichael of Edrom, Warden of the Middle Marches. Whether these are the original words, will admit of a doubt.'—*Scott.*

This is one of the songs which so touched Goldsmith in his youth that nothing he heard sung in after years had an equal charm for him. "The music of the finest singer," he wrote in the *Bee*, October 13, 1759, "is dissonance to what I felt when our old dairy-maid sung me into tears with Johnny Armstrong's Last Good-night, or the cruelty of Barbara Allen ;" and in a letter to his Irish friend Hodson, December 27, 1757, he says, "If I go to the opera where Signora Columba pours out all the mazes of melody, I sit and sigh for Lishoy's fireside, and Johnny Armstrong's Last Good-night from Peggy Golden."

GLOSSARY.

A, at, on; 'a fit,' *on foot.*
A', all; 'a' thing,' *everything.*
Abeigh, aside.
Aboon, Abune, above.
Acquaint, Acquent, acquainted.
Ae, one, only, sole, each, every.
Aff, off.
Afore, before.
Aften, often.
Aiblins, possibly, perhaps.
Aik, oak.
Ail, ailment.
Ain, own.
Air, early.
Airts (G. *örte*), points of the compass.
Aiten, oaten.
Aith (A. S. *áth*), oath.
Aits, oats.
Alane, alone.
Alang, along.
Amaist, almost.
Amang, among.
An, and, if.
Ance, once.
Ane, one.
Aneath, beneath.
Anither, another.
Arms, 'in arms,' *in each other's arms; arm-in-arm.*
Aside, beside.
Asklent, aslant.
Asse, ashes.

Asteer, astir, in a clatter, or ferment.
Athegither, all together, altogether.
A'thing, everything.
Athole-brose, whisky and oatmeal mixed together.
Atween, between.
Auld, old.
Auld - Mahoun (Mahomet) the Devil.
Ava, at all.
Awa, away.
Awee, a little; some time.
Aye, ever, always.
Ayont (A. S. *agcond*), beyond.

BA', ball.
Bailie, Magistrate of a Scotch Burgh, synonymous with *Alderman—Ritson.*
Bairn (*born*), child.
Baith, both.
Baloo, hush.
Ban, curse.
Bane (A. S. *bán*), bone.
Bang, beat, overcome.
Bannock, thick cake.
Barefit, barefoot, barefooted.
Baudrans, pet name for a cat (probably derived from the sound of her *purring*).
Bauk, balk; 'hen bauk,' *hen-roost.*
Bauld, bold, strong.

Bawsint, having a white mark on the brow.

Bedeen, immediately, at once, in a short time.

Befa' befall.

Bein, snug, warm and comfortable.

Belang, belong, belong to.

Beld, bald.

Bellowses, bellows.

Ben (*by-in*), within, in, inner part of a house. See But.

Benison, blessing.

Bent, the open country; coarse grass.

Benty, abounding in bent.

Bicker, a wooden vessel used for drinking ale.

Bide (A. S. *bidan*), abide, stay, endure

Biek, Beek (*lit.* bake), to bask.

Bield, Bielding, shelter.

Biggit, built.

Bigonet, linen cap or coif.

Billy, Billie, brother.

Bing, bin; 'corn-bing,' *corn-bin*.

Bing'd, curtsied.

Bink (G. *bank*), bench.

Birk, birch.

Birken, birchen.

Birkie, strutting, conceited fellow.

Birl, to spin round, to expend in drink.

Birns, stalks of burnt heather.

Bittle (A. S. *bitl*), beetle, heavy wooden mallet.

Blate (G. *blöde*), blushing, bashful.

Blaw, blow.

Blawn, blown.

Bleert, bleared.

Bleeze, blaze.

Blin', blind.

Blin (A. S. *blinnan*), cease.

Blink, glance, sparkle, twinkle.

Blude, Bluid, blood.

Blythesome, blithesome.

Bobbit, danced, moved up and down, ducked down, curtsied.

Bogie, dim. of bog.

Bogle, the game *hide and seek*.

Boued, bowed.

Bouir, bower.

Bowie (dim. of *bow*, bole), milk-pail.

Bracken (*brake*), fern; *Pteris aquilina.*

Brae, the side of a hill.

Brag, boast, crow over.

Braid, broad.

Braid, to plait.

Braird, first sprouting of sown grain.

Brak, broke.

Braw, brave, handsome, gallant, oftenest *well dressed.*

Brawlie, Brawly, beautifully, well.

Braws, finery.

Brecken, Breckan. See Bracken.

Bree, brow.

Bree (something brewed). juice, essence.

Breeks, breeches.

Breer, brier.

Breerie, briery.

Breist, breast.

Brent, smooth, unwrinkled; burnt.

Bricht, bright.

Brig, bridge.

Brocht, brought.

Broose, a tumultuous race at a country-wedding.

Brose, boiling water poured upon meal, formerly made with fat broth and oatmeal.

Bucht, Bught (G. *bucht*), little fold for inclosing ewes at milking-time.

Buchtin', Buchting, inclosing sheep in a fold.

Burn, Burnie, Burny, brook, rill, rivulet.

Burrow's-toun, burgh, corporate town.

Busk, dress, deck, prepare.

Buskit, Busket, dressed, decked.

But, without.

But, Butt (*by-out*), the kitchen; inferior, or outer part of a house ; ' but and ben,' *the outer and inner rooms of a house.*

Byre, cowhouse.

Ca', call, drive.

Ca'd, called, turned, put round.

Cadgily, jauntily.

Caller, cool, fresh, untainted,

Camsteery, Camsterry, perverse, quarrelsome.

Cankert, when applied to persons, ill-conditioned, thwarted, cross.

Canna, cannot.

Cannily, Cannilie, softly, gently, quietly.

Canny, Cannie, cautious, comfortable, gentle, knowing.

Canty (L. *canto*), disposed to sing, cheerful.

Carl, Carle, Carlic (A. S. *ceorl*), old man, churl.

Carline, old woman.

Castocks, cores or piths of cabbage stalks.

Cauf, calf.

Cauk, chalk.

Cauld, cold.

Cauldrife, chilly, sensitive to cold.

Cess, city-tax ; composition paid by the Scotch to freebooters for sparing their cattle, better known as *black mail—Ritson.*

Chackit, checked.

Chap, knock, strike ; ' chappit twal,' *struck twelve.*

Chappet-stocks, boiled cabbage.

Chappin, Chopin, a fluid measure of two English pints.

Cheery, cheerful.

Cheil, Chiel, childe, young man, fellow.

Chittering, shivering, trembling.

Christendie, Christendom.

Clachan, hamlet, little village.

Claes, Claise, clothes.

Clag, flaw, fault, failing.

Clamb (A. S. *climban, clamb*), climbed.

Clap, an instrument, used, instead of a bell, for making public proclamations.

Clash, gossip, idle rumour.

Clead, Cleed (G. *kleiden*), clothe.

Cleadin', Cleading, clothing.

Cleek, clutch, catch.

Clockin'-hen, clucking or hatching-hen.

Clout, blow, stroke ; patch, rag.

Coft (G. *gekauft*), bought.

Cog, Cogie, small wooden vessel without handles.

Coil, Coila, Burns' name for 'Kyle,' a district in Ayrshire.

Collie, Colly, Colin or shepherd's dog.

Coof, a simpleton, a contemptible fellow.

Coost, Cust, cast.

Cosy, Cosey, warm, snug, comfortable.

Couth, comfortable.

Crack, chat, talk.

Crackin', talking, chatting.

Craft, Croft, a field of kindly soil near the dwelling-house.

Craig (*dim.* Craigie, Craigy), crag, rock ; throat, neck.

Cramasie (Fr. *cramoisi*), crimson.

Crap (A. S. *cráp*), crept.

Craw, crow.

Crawflower, crowflower.

Creel, an ozier basket or Crhamper, made to be carried on the back.

eepie, low stool.

Croodle, to coo.

Crouse, brisk, smart, lively, triumphant.

Crowdy-mowdy, milk and meal boiled together.

Curchie (dim. of *curch*), a kerchief tied over the head to form a cap.

Cushat, ring-dove, wood-pigeon.

Cutty, short ; anything small ; a pretty name for the wren ; 'cutty-gun,' supposed to mean *tobacco-pipe*.

Daddet, thumped, struck violently.

Dadie, daddy, father.

Daff, to sport, to be gay, to play the fool.

Daffin', Daffing, foolish diversion, sport, absurd gaiety.

Daft, foolish, elated to giddiness.

Dander, Daunder, saunter, move about idly.

Daur, dare ; 'daurna,' *dare not*.

Daw, Dawing, dawn, dawning.

Dawtie, darling, pet, favourite.

Dawtit, cherished, caressed, fondled.

Deave, deafen.

Dee, die.

Deed, indeed.

Deid, dead, death ; 'deid-bell,' *passing bell*.

De'il, Devil.

Descriving, describing.

Deuk, duck ; 'deuk-dub,' duck puddle.

Didna, did not.

Dight, to wipe, to clean ; to winnow corn.

Dike. See Dyke.

Din, dun, sallow.

Ding, strike, beat, overcome in competition.

Dinna, do not.
Disna, does not.
Dochter, daughter.
Docken, dock.
Doited (dolted), grown stupid with age.
Dook (Fr. *doucher*), douse, duck, bathe.
Dool, ill-luck, sorrow ; an exclamation of pain or sorrow.
Do't, do it.
Douce, sober, wise, prudent.
Douff. See Dowf.
Doug, dog.
Doughtna, was not able to, could not.
Doune, Doun, down.
Doup, butt-end of anything.
Dour (Fr. *dur*), sullen; 'dour and din,' *sullen and sallow*.
Dow, dove.
Dow (Gr. *taugen*), can, is able.
Dowff, flaccid, spiritless.
Dowie, sad, doleful, melancholy.
Dozent, sleepy, benumbed, lifeless.
Draiglet, draggled.
Drap, drop.
Drave, drove.
Dribbles, drops ; 'nor dribbles of drink rins through the draff,' *i. e., no brewing goes on.*
Drift, something driven, as snow, dust, or the like.
Dringing, trilling.
Drookit, drenched.
Droun, drown.
Drouth, thirst, drought.
Drumly, muddy, disturbed, troubled.

Dub, a puddle, a little pool of water.
Duddy, ragged, tattered.
Duds, rags, clothes.
Dunt, stroke, blow, throb.
Durk, dirk, Highland dagger.
Dwallin', Dwalling, dwelling.
Dwine, Dwyne(A. S. *dwinan*), to dwindle, fade.
Dyke (G. *teich*), wall, hedge, ditch.

Earn, coagulate, curdle.
E'e, eye.
E'ed, eyed.
E'en, eyes ; even, evening.
E'ens, even as ; 'e'ens ye like,' *just as you like*.
Eerie, Earie, timorous, listening for supernatural sounds.
Eneugh, Eneuch, enough.
Ettle, intend, mean, aim.
Evened, paired, matched.
Ewe-buchts, sheepfolds.
Eke (A. S. *eac*), also.

Fa', chance, fate, luck.
Fa', fall ; 'fa' that,' *attempt that*.
Fa'en. See Faun.
Faes, foes.
Fairin', like English fairing ; also fare.
Fallow, fellow.
Fand, found.
Fare (A. S. *faran*), to go, to move forward; 'early fare,' *early march*.
Fash (Fr. *facher*), to trouble, to vex ; vexation, trouble.
Fashious, troublesome.
Fauld, fold.

Faun, fallen.
Fause, false.
Fecht (G. *fechten*), fight.
Feck (A. S. *fac*), quantity; 'monie feck,' *of much account*
Feckless, feeble, pithless, weak.
Feint, Fient, fiend; 'the feint a body,' *the devil a one.*
Fen, to make a shift, to scramble for a livelihood.
Ferlie, wonder.
'Fidging-fain,' *shaking with joy.*
Fiere, compeer, mate.
Fire-end, fire-side.
Fit, foot; 'aboon his fit,' *beyond his power.*
Flaffered, fluttered.
Flang, flung.
Flee, Flie, fly.
Fleech (Fr. *fléchir*), supplicate, pray.
Fleeching, coaxing, persuading by flattery.
Fleg, fright; frighten.
Fleyed, feared; 'needna fleyed,' *need not have been afraid.*
Flitting, change of abode; things *flitted.*
Flouris, flowers.
Fodgel, fat, squat, plump.
Fog, the generic name for moss, after-grass.
Forebears (forebe*ars*), ancestors.
Foreby, besides.
Forenent, opposite.
Forgather, encounter, meet.
Forlane, lonely, forlorn.
Forpet, fourth part of a peck.

Fou, Fu', full, tipsy.
Frae, from.
Frighted, frightened.
Funket, kicked, reared.
Fyle (A. S. *fulian*), to make dirty.

Gab, the mouth.
Gaberlunzie, a wallet which hangs on the side or loins.
Gaberlunzie-man, a wallet-man or tinker, who appears to have been formerly a jack-of-all-trades.—*Ritson.* Sometimes only called Gaberlunzie.
Gabbing, prating, talking pertly; speech coming only from the *gab.*
Gae, go, gave, give.
Gaed, Gade, Gaid, went.
Gane, gone.
Gane, Gain, suit, last, serve.
Gang, go.
Gar (Fr. *guerre*), compel, cause, force.
Gart, compelled, forced, caused.
Gat, got.
Gate, way, lane, habit.
Gaud (A. S. *gad*), goad; 'at the gaud,' *at the plough.*
Gaun, going.
Gawcie, jolly, large, buxom.
Gawdy, gaudy.
Gear, wealth, property.
Geck, to toss the head in disdain, to mock.
Gee (pron. *ghee*), the pet.
Genty (Fr. *gentil*), elegant, small, graceful.
Ghaist, ghost.
Gie, give; 'gie's,' *give us.*

Gied, gave.
Gif, Gin (*given*), if.
Gimmers, ewe-sheep under two years old.
Gimp, Jimp, slender.
Gir'd, hooped.
Girdle-cakes, oat cakes, baked over the fire on a *girdle*, or flat plate of iron.
Girn, to grin in anger.
Glaiket, idle, foolish, spell-bound.
Glamour, charm, spell.
Gleed, squinting.
Glen, a narrow valley between mountains.
Glent, glance, glitter, shine.
Gloaming, Gloamin' (A. S. *glomung*), twilight.
Glove, 'play at the glove,' *play at the glove-tilt.—Kitson.*
Glower, to glare, stare broadly.
Glum, gloomy, displeased.
Gorcock, moorcock.
Gouff'd, struck a blow (metaphor from the game of golf).
Goun, gown.
Gow, Neil Gow, a celebrated fiddler.
Gowan, field daisy, *Bellis perennis.*
Gowd, gold.
Gowdspink, goldfinch.
Gowk (*cuckoo*), simpleton, fool.
Grane, Grean, groan.
Grat, wept. See Greet.
Gree, degree, victory.
Gree (Fr. *gré*), agree.

Greet (A. S. *grætan*), weep.
Grunzie (Fr. *groin*, and *grogner*), snout, nose.
Gude, Guid, good.
Gudeman, goodman, husband; 'gudeman of day,' *the sun.*
Gudewife, wife, landlady.
Gude-willie, with good-will, cordial.
Gutcher, grandfather.

Ha', hall.
Hae, have; 'haena,' *have not.*
Haffet (Dan. *hoved*), the temple; 'gouff'd his haffet,' *slapped his face.*
Haflins, half.
Haill. See Hale.
Hained, saved, spared.
Haith (*Faith*), petty oath.
Hairst, harvest.
Hale, whole; 'hale-sale,' *wholesale.*
Hallanshaker, ragamuffin, sturdy beggar.
Halloween, 31st October, the Eve of Allhallows, the old superstitious rites connected with which are still celebrated in Scotland.
Hame, home.
Hand-breed, hand's breadth.
Hang, did hang, hung.
Hap, wrap, cover up.
Happer, hopper of a mill.
Happin, hopping.
Happity, hopping, lame.
Haud, hold.
Hauden, dwelling-house; holden, held.
Hawick-gill, a half mutchkin, double the ordinary gill.

Hawket-cow, white-faced cow.

Hawkies, white-faced cows, an affectionate name for cows in general.

Hecht, Heght, promised, engaged.

Herd (G. *hirte*), shepherd.

Herd, to tend, guard, watch.

Hereawa Thereawa, hitherward thitherward.

Heeze, hoist, raise, lift up.

Heezy, hoist, toss.

He's, he shall.

Hie, high.

Hielan', Hieland, highland.

Hill, ' at the hill,' *i.e., tending the sheep;* ' ta'en the hill,' *gone mad.*

Hind, beyond, behind.

Hing, hang.

Hirpling, halting, walking lame.

Hirsel, crawl.

Hizzie, Hussy, a goodnatured name for a buxom lively girl.

Hodden-gray, coarse woollen cloth of a gray colour.

Hool, hull, husk.

Hooly, softly, slowly.

Horn, drinking-horn.

Hout, an exclamation like ' Tush.'

Howe, hollow.

Hun', Hund (G. *hund*), dog ; ' hund the tykes,' *incite the dogs to keep the sheep together.*

Hunder, hundred.

Hurklin', crouching, cowering.

Hurry-burry, hurly-burly.

Hussyffskap, housewifery, housewifeship.

Hynd, hind.

Ilk, Ilka (A. S. *ylc*), same, every; ' that ilk,' *that same.*

Ill-far'dly, ill-favouredly, unbecomingly.

In, into.

Ingle, fire.

Into, in.

Irk, to grow weary.

I'se, I shall or will.

Ither (A. S. *äther*), other, each other.

Ithers, others, each others.

' It's no,' it shall not, it is not.

Jade, Jaud, a rather kindly name for a mischievous girl.

Jag, the best part of calfleather.

Jee, to move aside, sway, vibrate.

Jimp, slender, neat.

Jimply, neatly, tightly.

Jo, Joe, sweetheart, darling.

Jouk (G. *ducken*), to duck, evade, bow, stoop.

Jow, jolt, knell ; ' it includes both the swinging motion and pealing sound of a large bell.'—*Burns.*

Kail, Kale, colewort; broth.

Kail-yard, kitchen-garden.

Kame (G. *kämmen*), comb.

Kebbuck, cheese.

Keckling, cackling.

Keek (G. *gucken*), to peep ; ' keeking-glass,' *lookingglass.*

Keekit, peeped.

Keel, red-ochre.

Keen (G. *kuhn*), ardent, brave.

Ken, to know, to be acquainted with.

Kent, a long staff used by shepherds for leaping ditches.

Kent, Kenned, knew, known.

Kill, kiln.

Kimmer, gossip, wife, married woman.

Kintra, country.

Kirn, churn.

Kist (A. S. *cyst*), chest.

Kit, a little wooden vessel hooped and staved.

Kittle (G. *kitzelig*), ticklish, ticklishly.

Knaws, knows.

Knowe, knoll, hillock.

Kurch, Curchie (old Fr. *couvrechef*), kerchief tied over the head instead of a cap.

Ky, Kye, cows.

Kyle, a district in Ayrshire.

LAG, hindmost.

Laigh, low; a low field reclaimed from a marsh; the undrainable portion of a farm.

Lair, Lear (A.S. *laer*), learning, lore.

Laird, landlord, proprietor of land or houses.

Laith, loath, unwilling.

Lammie, lambkin.

Lane, Lain, alone; 'her lane,' *by herself.*

Lang, long; ' or lang,' *ere long.*

Lang-kail, 'pottage made of coleworts.'—*Ritson.*

Langsome, tedious.

Lave, the remainder, the rest.

Laverock, Lavrock, lark.

Law, low.

Lawing, tavern reckoning.

Lawlands, lowlands.

Lay, allay, alleviate, exorcise

Lea', leave.

Leal, loyal, honest, true.

Lear. See Lair.

Learns (G. *lehren*), teaches.

Lee, lea.

Leelang, live-long.

Leesome (*liefsome*), happy, joyous.

Leeze me (probably *lief's me*, like *weed's me*), dear is to me.

Leglin, a wooden milking-pail.

Leuch, Leugh, laughed.

Lib, shear, p. 264.

Licht, light.

Lick, a wag, cheat, one who plays tricks.

Lift (A. S. *lyft*), air, sky, firmament.

Lig, lie.

Lightlie, jeer, despise, mock.

Lightsome, cheerful.

Lilt, to sing, to sing in recitative.

Limmer, slut; 'an opprobrious term applied to young women, expressive of displeasure, but not implying immorality of conduct.'—*Ritson.*

Link, to step lightly and nimbly.

Linn, a waterfall, cascade, precipice covered with brushwood.

Lint-white, linnet.

Loaning, loan, lane, where in summer the cows are milked.

Lo'ed, Loo'd, loved.

Loof, palm of the hand.

Loot, did let.

Losh (*Lord*), petty oath.

Loup, leap.

Loupin', Louping, leaping.

Loun, Loon, rogue, rascal, worthless fellow.

Lout (A. S. *lútan*), to bow, stoop.

Lowe, flame.

Luck, to prosper.

Lucken-gowan, the globe flower, *Trollius Europæus*.

Lyart (A. S. *ħe*, locks, and *ħár*, hoar), hoary headed.

Mae, more.

Mahoun (Mahomet), the devil.

Mailing (A. S. *mæl*), rented farm.

Main, Mane, moan.

Mainteen, maintain.

Mair (G. *mehr*), more.

Maist, most.

Maister, master.

Mak', make.

Mark. See Merk.

Marrow, mate, companion.

Martinmas: in Scotland servants are engaged by the half-year, 'Whitsunday' and 'Martinmas' being the two terms. p. 90.

Mat (A. S. *mót*), may, must.

Maukin, hare.

Maun, must; 'maunna, *must not.*

Maut, malt.

Maw, mow.

May, maiden.

Mear, mare.

Meikle, much, large, big.

Mense, to grace; 'into the mense,' *into the bargain.*

Men't, mended.

Merk, ancient Scottish coin, value one shilling and fourpence farthing, English.

Micht, might.

Midden-creels, panniers in which horses carry manure.

Milk-bowie, a shallow milking-pail.

Milket, milked.

Min', Mind, remind, remember.

Minnie, Minny, mother.

Mint, was minded, meant.

Mirk (A. S. *myrc*), dark.

Monie, Mony, many.

Morn, 'the morn,' *to-morrow.*

Mou', mouth.

Mouter, the miller's mulct or due for grinding grain.

Muckle. See Meikle.

Muir, moor.

Mune, moon.

Mutch (G. *mütze*), woman's linen cap.

Na, no, not.

Nae, none, no.

Naething, nothing.

Nagy, Nagie, Naigie, little nag, pony; 'shanks-naggie,' *on his own feet.*

Napkin, pocket handker-
chief.
Nappie, Nappy, ale; to be
tipsy.
Nane, none.
Neebours, neighbours.
Neist, next.
Neive, Nieve, fist.
Neivefu', handful.
Neep, turnip.
Neuk, nook, corner.
Nicht, night.
Nocht, Nought, nothing.
Nookit, cornered.
Notour, notorious.

Ocht, Aught, anything.
Oercome. See Owerword.
Ony, any.
Or, ere, before.
O't, of it.
Out-owre, over.
Ower, over.
Owerword, burden of a song.
Owrlay, cravat.
Owsen, Ousen, oxen.
Oxter, arm-pit, 'in his oxter,'
under his arm.

Paidle, paddle, patrol, walk
with short childish steps.
Parritch, oatmeal porridge.
In the mouth of the people,
'parritch' is almost uni-
versally spoken of in the
plural, as is also barley
broth, *i.e.,* 'They're round
about the feetie o't,' p. 242.
Pat, pot.
Pat, put.
Pawky, sly, shrewd, knowing.
Pearlings, apparellings, ap-
parel.

Peat-pat, the hole from which
the peat is dug.
Pendles, pendants, earrings.
Philabeg, Highland kilt.
Pickle, a grain of corn, a
single seed of any kind, a
small quantity.
Piece, way, distance.
Pits, puts.
Plack, ancient Scotch coin,
value a third of a penny,
English.
Plaiden, a thick woollen stuff
for making plaids; 'plaid-
ing coat,' *coarse woollen
petticoat.*
Pleen, complain.
Plenished, furnished, stocked.
Pleuch, Pleugh, plough.
Poortith, poverty.
Pou, pull; Pou'd, pulled.
Pouther, powder.
Pow, poll, pate.
Prie, try, taste, prove.
Priving, proving, trying, tast-
ing.
Pu', pull; Pu'in', Pu'ing,
pulling.
Puir, poor.
Putted, threw; 'putted the
stane,' *threw the stone,* a
game for proving strength.

Quat, quit, quitted.
Quean (queen, in its primary
signification) woman, young
woman.
Quey (Icel. *kviga*), young
cow.
Quo', quoth.

Rackit, racked, stretched.
Rade, rode.

Raired (A. S. *reord*), made a clangour.
Raise, Rase, rose.
Randy, a shrew, a boisterous, ill natured person.
Rang, reigned.
Ranting-fire, roaring fire.
Ranty-tanty, 'the broad-leaved sorrel, *Rumex acetosella*, which was boiled with colewort and beat up together.'—*Ritson.*
Reaming, foaming, frothing.
Reca', recall.
Rede (G. *reden*), speak, advise.
Red-up, Redd-up, tidy, neat.
Reest, to become restive.
Richt, right.
Rift, to eructate, belch.
Rigs, Riggs, ridges.
Rin, run; Rinnin', running.
Rippling-kame, a coarse comb used for separating the flax from the stalks.
Rock, distaff.
Rockley, Rokely, (G. *röcklein*, short cloak.
Row, roll, wrap.
Roosed, praised, admired.
Roset, shoemakers' wax.
Rowan, berry of the mountain ash; the mountain ash.
Runkled, wrinkled.

Sabbin', Sabbing, sobbing.
Sae, so, thus.
Saft, soft.
Sair (G. *sehr*), sore, much.
Sairly, Sarely, sorely.
Sairs, serves.
Sall, shall.
Sang, song.

Sark, shirt, chemise.
Saugh, willow.
Saul! petty oath (*by my soul*).
Saunt, saint.
Saut, salt.
Saxpence, sixpence.
Sayed, essayed, tried.
Scad, scald.
Scantly, scantily, hardly, scarcely.
Scauldin', Scaulding, scolding.
Scone, a small soft cake common in Scotland.
Screen,—'*tartan-screen*', a large scarf forming a kind of plaid.
Scrimp, to stint, to deal out in a niggardly way.
Scug, shelter, ward off, defend.
Sel', self.
Set (A. S. *settan*), appoint, fix; appointed, fixed.
Seugh, furrow, ditch.
Sey, a kind of woollen stuff.
Shanks (A. S. *sceanca*), legs.
'Shanks-nagy,' euphemism for walking.
Shanna, shall not.
Shaw, a wood, plantation, woody bank.
Shearing, reaping, harvest.
Sheughing, planting.
Sheuk, shook.
She's, she is, she shall.
Shiel, a temporary shed for shepherds on the mountains.
Shoon, shoes.
Shoulter, shoulder.
Shure, shore, sheared, reaped.
Shyre, sheer, 'as shyre a lick,' *as bright a cheat.*

Sie, Siccan (A. S. *swylc*), such.

Siller, silver, money.

Simmer, summer.

Sin, since; Sinsyne, since then.

Sith (A. S. *sithan*), since.

Skaith, hurt, damage, injury, undoing.

Skaithless, unhurt.

Skirling, shrieking, screaming.

Slaes, sloes.

Slawly, slowly.

Slee, sly.

Sleigh, sly.

Slippit, slipped, glided.

Sma', small; 'linen sae small,' *linen so fine.*

Smiddy (G. *schmiede*), smithy.

Smoor (A. S. *smoran*), smother.

Sna', Snaw, snow.

Snell (G. *schnell*), keen, sharp, piercing.

Snood, ribbon for the hair. See p. 228, n.

Sonsy, Sonsey, buxom, well-favoured, blooming.

Sough, sigh, dreary sound made by the wind among trees.

Soum, relative number of sheep or cattle to a pasture; ten, and sometimes five.

Soup, Sowp, sip, small quantity of anything fluid.

Souple, supple.

Souter, cobbler, shoemaker.

Spak, spoke.

Speer, Spier (A. S. *spirian*), to ask, inquire.

Spill, spoil, destroy.

Spindles and Whorles, implements used in spinning with the distaff.

Stack, peat-stack.

Stack, stuck.

Staukin', stalking.

Staw, stole.

Sten, Stenn, start, leap.

Stended, started.

Stented, stinted.

Steer, stir, move, touch, injure.

Stirk (A. S. *styrc*), young bull.

Stoun, Stown, stolen; 'could stown,' *could have stolen.*

Stound, throb, sudden pang.

Stoup, deep vessel for liquids, a measure for spirits, &c., as gill-stoup, pint-stoup.

Strae, straw.

Strakit, struck.

Strang, strong; strung.

Strath, valley.

Strathspey, a dance, so called from the district in which it originated.

Streek, stretch, extend.

Strick, strict.

Sturt, strife, trouble, vexation.

Styme, glance.

Sumph, lout.

Sune, soon.

Swankies (*swainkins*), lively young fellows.

Swats, new ale, small ale.

Syke, a rill, usually dry in summer time.

Syne, then, since, ago; 'Lang syne,' *long ago.*

Ta'en, taken.

Tap, top; 'tap to tae,' *top to toe.*

Tappit-hen, crested hen; Scotch quart-measure, so called from a knob on the lid.

Tapsalteerie, topsy-turvy.

Tassie (Fr. *tasse*), cup.

Tauk, talk.

Tauld, told.

Taylor, tailor.

Temper-pin, a wooden pin for regulating the motion of a spinning-wheel.

Tent, tend, attend, heed.

Thae (A. S. *thá*), these, those.

Thanket, thanked.

Theek (G. *decken*), thatch.

Theekit, thatched.

Thegither, together.

They'se, they shall.

Thir, these.

Thocht, thought.

Thoom, thumb.

Thowe, thaw.

Thowless (*dowless*), helpless, inert, lazy, without power. See Dow.

Thrang, (G. *dringen*), busy, crowded.

Thraw, throw, twist, 'thraw their neck about,' *i.e., kill.*

Thrawn, ill-conditioned, cross, ill-natured.

Thretty, thirty.

Thysell, Thysel', thyself.

Tichtly, tightly, completely.

Tiff, order.

Till, to, until.

Tine, Tyne, loss, die.

Tint, lost.

Tintock-tap, the top of Tinto, a high hill in Lanarkshire.

Tippenny, twopenny; ale sold at 2d. the Scotch pint.

Tirl, twirl; 'tirl the sneck,' *twirl the latch.*

Tither, other.

Titty, sister.

Tocher, properly Tocher-Gude (G. *Tochtergut*), marriage-portion, fortune.

Todlin', toddling.

Toom (part. of old Eng. *tem*), empty.

Toomed, emptied, poured out.

Toun, town; also farm or inclosed land (G. *zaun*).

Toys, head-dresses.

Trews, breeches.

Trig, compact, neat.

Trinkling, trickling, waving.

Troth, Trowth, truth, indeed.

Trow, to believe, to be certain, to trust to, to confide in.

Tryste, appointment; also a fair.

Tull, to.

Twa, two.

Twal, twelve.

Twin, Twine, to part, separate, divide.

Twin'd, Twinned, parted, separated.

Tyne. See Tine.

Tyke, an opprobrious name for a dog.

Unco, Unca (un-*quoth*), strange, very wonderful.

Uneasy, not easy, difficult.

Unfauld, unfold.

VAUNTY, boastful, vain.

WABSTER (webster), weaver.
Wad, would; Wadna, would not.
Wae (A. S. *wa*), woe, sad; 'wae's me,' *woe is me*.
Waefu', Waeful, woeful.
Waesome, woeful.
Waladay, well-a-day.
Wale (G. *wählen*), choose, select.
Walie, large, ample.
Walloch, 'a kind of dance familiar to the Highlands,' —*Jamieson*.
Waly (waely), an exclamation of grief; sadly, woefully.
Wame, belly.
Wan, pale.
Wan, won, got, gained.
Ware, to spend, expend, bestow.
Wark, work,
Warl, Warld, world; Warly, worldly.
Warlock (A. S. *wærloga*), wizard; 'Warlock-knowe,' *knoll supposed to be frequented by warlocks*.
Warsle, wrestle, struggle.
Warst, worst.
Wast, west.
Wat (A.S. *witan. he wait*, he knows), know, believe, declare.
Wat, wet.
Waught, deep draught.
Wauken, waken.
Wauking, waking, awake.
Wauk, walk; to shrink as fuller's thicken cloth.

Weans (*wee ones*), children.
Wear (G. *wehren*), drive, gather together partly by force.
Wearifu', wearisome, vexatious.
Wedders, wethers.
Wede, weeded.
Wee, small, little; 'a wee,' or 'awee,' a short while.
Weel, Weil, well; 'weel's me on,' *well is to me on* (*I am delighted with*).
Weet, wet.
Weir, war.
We'se, we shall.
Westlin, westerly.
Wha, Whae, who; Wha-e'er, whoever; Wham, whom.
Whang, slice, slash, large piece slashed off.
Whar, Whare, where.
Whiles, Whyles, at times, occasionally.
Whilk, which.
Whinging, whining.
Whisht, hush,
Whorles. See Spindles.
Widow, widow, widower.
Wilily, slyly, cunningly.
Wiltu, wilt thou.
Win, to earn, to get.
Winna, will not.
Winsome, winning, comely, engaging.
Wiss'd, wished.
Wist (A. S. *witan*), knew, know; 'wistna,' *knew not*.
Wi't, with it.
Withershins, contrary to the course of the sun.

Witless, unheeding, unsuspecting.

Wob, web.

Won (G. *wohnen*), dwell, live.

Woo, wool.

Wow, (*I vow*), an exclamation denoting eagerness or surprise.

Wraith, ghost, spirit, apparition.

Wrak (*wreck*), confusion, vexation.

Wud (G. *wuth*), mad, distracted.

Wylie, wily.

Yad, Yade, Yaud, jade, mare.

Yaird, Yard, Yairdie, Yardie, garden, little garden.

Yammer (G. *jammern*), to murmur, whimper, whine.

'Ye'd thought,' *you would have thought.*

Ye'se, you shall.

Yestreen (yestereven), last night.

Yet (A. S. *geat*), gate.

Yill, ale.

Yowes, ewes.

Yule, Christmas.

Yumphing, noise made by dogs in hunting.

INDEX OF WRITERS.

WITH DATES OF BIRTH AND DEATH

INDEX OF TITLES.

INDEX OF FIRST LINES.